Ransom Slave

First Edition

Published by The Nazca Plains Corporation
Las Vegas, Nevada
2008

ISBN: 978-1-934625-84-2

Published by
The Nazca Plains Corporation ®
4640 Paradise Rd, Suite 141
Las Vegas NV 89109-8000

PUBLISHER'S NOTE
Ransom Slave is a work of fiction created wholly by *Richard Andrews'* imagination. All characters are fictional and any resemblance to any persons living or deceased is purely by accident. No portion of this book reflects any real person or events.

Cover, Fleshblack
Art Director, Blake Stephens

Dedication

I would like to dedicate this story to all the close friends in the leather community that I have lost in the last few decades to the killer that is referred to as AIDS. My life was greatly enriched by their presence and I miss them dearly.

Richard Andrews

Ransom Slave

First Edition

Richard Andrews

Table of Contents

Chapter 1:

JAMES

The bus trip from Indiana to Los Angeles was long and boring, with a stop at almost every small and large town on the way. I felt a great sign of relief after the bus driver announced that we were only about one twenty miles outside of L.A. The boredom of the trip and the problem of having to try to sleep in an uncomfortable bus seat was almost over.

As the bus approached the bus station a sense of fear started to grip me. What was going to happen to me in this new and very strange city? I was an 18 year old, gay boy from a small town in Indiana and I didn't know jack about how to live and survive in a major city.

As the bus pulled up to the station my hands began to shack a little. This was not the first time that I have had a problem with dealing with fear. When ever a big change in my life takes place, or I had a major problem, I would sometimes get the shacks and have to sit down until my body started to relax. Sometimes the fear would get so intense that I would have to sit on the floor, with my back against the wall, with my arms around my folded legs and just cry. Danger and

1

change were the facts of life that I still have a problem adjusting too.

My problem with fear probably had something to do with the fact that my parents were killed in a car accident when I was just 10 years old. At least that is when the problem started. After the death of my parents I lived in a number of foster homes and group homes for the last 8 years. They were called homes, but none of them really felt like home to me.

After the bus had stopped I started to get my stuff together. I was traveling light I only had a coat and a small overnight bag. I guess you can say that I am a poor boy with very little to call my own. The only thing that I have that you could call a valuable asset is my body. It is the only thing that I have gotten out of life that seems to have any real value.

Having a good looking body and big dick is the only reason that I actually got noticed at all during the time I was growing up in Indiana. My personality certainly never got me many points as a boy or teenager. I am a shy person and I tend to be a loner. I never socialized much in school and I had few friends. The only time people paid any real attention to me was when I was naked. I was on several teams in high school and I always got stared at in the showers. At the time I thought the whole scene was rather funny, all those horny straight guys in school wanted to fuck my pretty ass, but their own code of conduct wouldn't let them. So, I guess they just had to go home and beat off or something.

I knew that I was attracted to guys from an early age, but in the fag hating schools I went to I stayed very much in the closet. The only real sexual experience that I had was a six month relationship with an older foster brother. Well, I call it a relationship, but in fact I was more like his sex slave. He used my mouth and ass for his pleasure every day. I had no complaints. This fact would go a long ways in explaining why I took a bus to L.A. right after I finished high school. I just got fed up with the whole fag hating town. Not that they just hated fags they hated a long list of people, blacks, Hispanics, liberals, commies etc. etc. All that I really knew was that I didn't belong in my home town anymore. I just had to get out and find where I really belonged in this crazy world

About the time I walked into the bus station my hands had stopped shacking and my mood started to change for the better. The weather in L.A. was bright and sunny and the station was packed with people. As I walked down the main corridor I was suddenly jolted to one side as a young man ran in to me and I dropped my overnight bag. The young man said, "I'm sorry man, are you all right?" I picked up my bag and checked my wallet, I still had it. I had heard stories about pickpockets and I had to check.

"Yes, I'm O.K." As I turned to look at the young man, I looked directly into his eyes. He was about in his mid twenties I would say and ruggedly good looking. You could say that he was just my type. From that moment on being to thrusting was my downfall. That attractive face and beautiful eyes caused my dick to start to get hard and I quickly started to make bad decisions.

As I stood there with my mouth open the young man knew that he had me and all he needed to do is reel me in. "Well, it seems that no real harm was done, but if you will let me I would like to buy you a cup of coffee to make up for being so rude." I quickly agreed and he introduced himself. "My name is Brad, what is yours?" "My parents named me James, but people just call me Jimmy." "Well, Jimmy it is. Follow me, there is a diner in the station." As I followed Brad I started to look him over, well at least his backside. He was well dressed with broad shoulders and a nice looking ass. I felt like I had just lucked out big time. I could only think over and over again that I hoped that he was gay.

The cup of coffee really hit the spot. After a long and boring trip it felt good to talk to someone who seemed to actually be interested in me. There was something about Brad that brought me out of my shell. After only about an hour and two cups of coffee Brad had pretty much heard my life story and he seemed to really be interested in me. Being in the closet in a small fag hating town for so long had made me an easy mark for a guy like Brad, but I did not know it at the time.

Brad offered me a place to stay until I got on my feet. I was fascinated by Brad and basically scared of this the big new city that I now found myself in. Brad seemed to me to be an experienced man of the world type and I started to feel safe around him. I was sort of shuck dumb by his good looks and his knowledge of this new L.A. world that I had chosen to live in. It did not occur to me to ask Brad why a good looking, well-built, young man, who drove a new BMW, was doing hanging around the bus station. I was young and very experienced in the ways of the big city world. All I could think of was how I was going to get a chance to ball Brad. I hadn't had any sex in six months and I was as horny as hell. My half hard dick was doing the thinking for me and all that I wanted to do is to slowly lick every inch of Brad's naked body, give him the best blow job of his life and get royally fucked.

Brad's house was in the Hollywood Hills, on a tree lined street, over looking the city. The house was a one story Spanish style home with a red tile porch. As we entered the front hallway I could see that the house had a pool in the back yard, surrounded by a beautiful garden. The house took my breath away they don't have houses like this where I came from, not ever close.

Brad told me to just put my stuff on the sofa in the living room and to get naked. I didn't even stop to think why he wanted me naked, I only knew that I wanted his body and showing him my naked body seemed like a great way to get him interested. After all no one had ever told me that I had a bad looking body.

When Brad walked out of the kitchen he had two glasses of wine in his hands. He stopped for a brief moment and he stared wide eyed at me. I smiled, it seemed that I was about to score, Brad definitely liked what he saw. Brad gave me one of the glasses of wine as his eyes inspected my naked body. With out saying a word he walked around me, looking me over, as I took a few sips of wine.

"God damn, you really have a great looking body and one hell of a big dick. Just looking at you has me so turned on I feel like picking you up and taking you to my bed and making love to every inch of you and that's just for starters." I put my glass down on the coffee table and walked over to stand in front of Brad. As I stared into his beautiful eyes I put my arms around his shoulders and I gave him a slow, deep kiss as I felt his hands move down my back and grasp my bare ass. As I withdrew my lips from his he firmly grabbed both my ass cheeks, lifted me off the ground and said, "Well boy, do you want to find out how they ball in L.A.?" I just smiled, "Any time that you are ready."

Brad did not say a word, he just put his put one arm around my shoulders, bent over and cupped the back of my legs with the other and lifted me up off the ground. The feel of this powerful young man picking me up had my big cock hard and throbbing in just a few seconds. I didn't care about what made sense any more I just knew that I wanted Brad.

Just after Brad carried me into his bedroom, he put me down in an over stuffed chair, just before he walked over to a sound system and put a tape in the machine. He now turned to face me and said, "Well sweet cheeks you gave me a nice little show in the living room, now it's my turn." With that he turned on the play button. As the tape began to play he started to do a slow strip tease act. I did not say a word I just sat there watching Brad slowly take off each piece of his clothing as my big cock throbbed up and down on my stomach.

Brad's strip act lasted about 15 minutes and I sat there wide-eyed, with my month slightly open, as his shirt came off, revealing a very muscular and well-defined torso that was well accented by two very developed arms. Next he kicked off his shoes and pulled off his socks, before he started to play a little game with his pants and underwear. He slowly unzipped his pants and let them drop to the ground, before he began to play a slow cock teasing game with his jockey shorts.

Finally, Brad took his underwear off, revealing a half hard 8 inch cock, very muscular legs and a nice firm rounded ass. As Brad started to run his hands over his naked body I was starting to breathe harder, I was so turned on that I felt like shooting my load all over my chest and stomach, right than an there.

I know that I had to have him and as the music was ending I got up and walked over to Brad and got down on my knees and begged him for his cock. "Please Sir, may I suck your cock?" Brad didn't answer, the music stopped and he bent over and ran his hands over my back down to my ass and back again. My mouth just watered as his pulsating cock landed right in my face.

"Well, so you want to play." Brad now stood up and grabbed his hard cock, exposing his firm and hairless balls and said, "Well sweet cheeks lets see you earn my cock. Lick my balls boy." "Yes Sir!"

I didn't need any more encouragement I leaned forward and with my warm, moist tongue I started to tongue massage his balls. As I licked his balls from one side to the next Brad began to mildly moan and his legs began to shake. His reaction to my tongue bath only encouraged me to lick faster, as his moaning and shaking grow more intense.

The scent of his crotch and his approving moans had my cock throbbing wildly up and down. I was so turned on that I felt like a dog in heat and I hadn't even got to suck dick yet.

Just as I thought that I was about to get to suck Brad's cock, I felt a hand grab the back of my head as I heard Brad say, "Get up boy, it's time for some pec work." After I stood up my head was pushed on to Brad's chest and I was told to get to work. I eagerly started to lick Brad's right nipple as he played with my cock and balls. After only a few minutes of licking his nipples, Brad raised his right arms and he forced my head over to work on his pit. I licked around the sides of his arm pit and than the center. Brad moaned loudly and I started to breathe harder, as if I was getting close to cumming.

Suddenly, Brad pulled me off his chest, just as he grabbed the head of my cock and squeezed it really hard. I just stood there, face to face with Brad, until my cock settled down. Brad than let go of my cock and gave me a long slow kiss before he put me back to work licking his nipples and pits.

After Brad seemed very satisfied with my performance I was told to get on my knees. The thought that I was finally going to get Brad's dick had my cock going wild and I was starting to breathe faster again. The idea of getting to suck his big cock and maybe even taste his warm, sweet cum, was starting to do a trip on my head.

As I got to my knees, Brad put his hands on the sides of my head, so that I could not move, just as he positioned his cock on my nose and forehead and his balls on my lips. "Now Boy, I want you to lick one side of my cock and than the other, than I want you to deep throat my cock, one stroke after another, until I shoot a big load down your throat. Do you understand, Boy?" I just moved my head up and down, rubbing his cock and balls in my face.

When Brad backed away from me I quickly started to lick his cock, until it was completely wet. As I slowly swallowed his cock, clean down to his hair, he let out a loud moan and his whole body shook a little. As I continued to deep tongue his cock his moans grow louder. The more that he moaned and his body shook the more turned on I became.

His reactions to my little performance only encouraged me to suck faster as he started to build to climax. Just before he came he let out a loud moan, as he grabbed the back of my head and forced his cock down my throat. He moaned loudly one more time as his cock swelled and he started to pump a big load of warm, sweet cum down my throat. I gagged a little at first, but my throat quickly adjusted as I drank the steady stream of man cum, right down to the last drop.

After Brad had shoot his load I cleaned off the last drops of cum from his cock with my tongue. I had not had any man sex in almost 6 months and sucking off Brad had been just like having the best tasting dessert that I've ever had. I only wish that I could have sucked him off 10 times in a row.

Brad wasn't going to let me suck him off again, well not just yet, he had other plans for his cock. Brad bent over and put his hands under my armpits and lifted me up to my feet. He than put his arms around me and gave me a long slow kiss.

After several minutes of deep, warm kisses, Brad stopped and looked into my eyes as his hands grabbed my ass cheeks. "Now Boy, you have proven to be such a turn-on that I just have to fuck you." I just smiled. Brad smiled too, just before he walked over to the bed and threw back the covers and than placed two pillows on top of each other in the middle of the bed. I don't need to be told what to do I just got on the bed face down with the pillows under my hips and relaxed.

When my body started to relax I felt Brad's hands run up and down my naked body, just before I felt a hand slap my bare ass really hard. My body reacted to the blow by tensing up for a few seconds before I relaxed again and I started to eagerly wait for the feel of a greased man cock sliding up my ass.

As I waited, Brad walked over to a desk and got out a jar and several towels. He than walked over in back of me and I felt several fingers start to play with the crack of my ass. The slow massaging nature of Brad's fingers soon had my body mildly shacking. Than suddenly, I felt two hands part my ass cheeks and I could feel the warm, wet feel of a tongue starting to rim my ass. I felt so good I started to moan and my legs shook.

After only a few minutes of what I would call expert rimming, my body had completely relaxed, just before I felt a hard, greased cock slid deep into my ass in one fast stroke.

The force of the deep thrust of Brad's cock caused my upper body to lift off the bed and I let out a loud moan. The next few thrusts were slow and deep and my ass quickly adjusted to the feel of a man's cock inside of me. I started to moan and squirm as the pleasure of being fucked by a stud man started to really turn me on. Soon, Brad put his hands on my shoulders and really started to shove it to me, long and deep. This new method had me moaning and squirming in no time.

Just as I was showing signs of getting close to climax Brad backed off and my body started to relax. It seems that Brad understood my body as well as I and he didn't want me to cum just yet.

When my body stopped shacking and I was breathing at a more normal rate, Brad turned me over on my back, put my legs on his shoulders and he started to really shove it to me again. It only took a few minutes to get me squirming and moaning again as I got close to cumming. But, this time was different, Brad smiled and said, "Now Boy lets see you cum without touching yourself." I smiled one last time, before I started to shot a big load all over myself. As my cock unloaded, Brad pulled his cock out of my ass and just let it freely shot a warm load of warm, sticky cum on my chest and stomach.

Brad looked very pleased with me. "Boy that was the best sex I have had in a long time. You are really something." With that he grabbed several towels and he cleaned up the both of us before he pulled me up off the bed and said, "O.K. sweet cheeks lets take a shower. After the shower we went shinny dipping in the backyard pool. He felt good to swim naked in a heated pool and make out with Brad again. When we finished our swim we went back into the bedroom to rest. As Brad laid down next to me I turned over on my side and put my arms around him with my head on his chest. He put one arm across my back and said, "Boy lets get a little sleep." I don't any more encouragement as we both relaxed and drifted off to sleep.

Chapter 2:

A NEW LIFE

Sleeping in the nude with Brad, that first night, was the most comfortable nights sleep that I can remember ever having. The warmth of his muscular body and soft sound of his beating heart made me feel very content and for the first time in my life I felt protected and safe. I didn't know much about life, especially in the big city, I only knew that I liked this feeling and I wanted it to continue.

I awoke the next morning laying on my back, with a warm, wet feeling in my groin. I opened my eyes to see that the bed covers were off the bed, and Brad was giving me a slow blow job, my body started to tense-up.

Just as Brad realized that I was awake he deep throated my stiff cock, clear down to my hair and slowly sucked his way back up, until he was slowly licking the head of my cock. The sensation felt soon good that I let a loud moan and my legs shook. Brad grabbed my cock, looked at me and smiled as he started to slowly beat me off with his hand. "Well good morning sweet cheeks." He did not say anymore he just eagerly started to lick my balls as he continued to beat me off.

The dual sensation of Brad's warm, moist tongue, eagerly massaging my balls, while his hand stroked my cock, had me near climax in no time. I started to moan real loud, my body started to squirm. I could not stop it I was going to cum. As my cock unloaded several streams of warm, sticky cum, several feet into the air above the bed, I almost screamed. As cum splashed down on me and the bed Brad started to stroke my cock even faster as he continued to lick my balls and my body violently shook.

As soon as my cock started to relax and my body stopped violently shaking, Brad stopped stroking my cock and leaned forward and put his hands on each side of my chest. He looked directly into my eyes and smiled, "Well, you don't think that you are the only one who likes to suck dick, did you?" I just smiled and all I could think of saying was, "Thank you that was the best wake-up call that I have ever had."

Brad gave me a long, deep kiss and than he leaned back and sat on his legs. His eyes looked over my cum covered body and laughed a little, "Wow, you can sure shoot a big load. You must be the most cum filled boy in the country."

With that Brad took me by the hands and pulled me off the bed. He put his arms around me with his hands on my ass cheeks. Brad squeezed my ass really hard and said, "Well Boy get ready, today we are going to the beach." I smiled and said nothing. In the mood that I was in I would do anything Brad wanted me to do.

It took us only about an hour to shower and eat breakfast and we were out the door. Brad gave me a pair of walking shorts, a football jersey, some new tennis shoes and a pair of expensive looking sunglasses to wear. Before we left I looked myself over in a full length mirror. I looked good almost like I belonged in sunny California.

The trip to Black's Beach in San Diego was going to take several hours and I looked forward to learning more about Brad. I had told Brad my life story at the bus station, but I still did not know much about him or his life, except that he really turned me on and made me feel safe and comfortable.

As we hit the highway I wanted to ask Brad a few questions. But before I could open my mouth Brad started to ask questions. "Well Boy, what do you plan to make a living while you are in L.A.?" "Actually, I didn't know. I only have experience in fast food and waiting on tables. Nothing that pays all that good, you can say that I have very few real skills."

Brad smiled at me and said, "Well Boy, you my have lucked out when I bumped into you at the bus station, maybe I can set you up with a decent paying job and interesting life. "What do you mean? What type of good paying job would I be qualified for?

"Well, you can let me manage your life. You can be my boy." I didn't know what he meant. Hell, I did not know much about him. But, the part about being his boy sounded really good.

"Can you explain what you mean a little better?" Brad smiled and said, "Boy, I run a small firm production company. I make gay porn films, manage a male escort business and I am considered to be a major gay porn star." It suddenly hit me, Brad was Chuck Wade. I had seen him in several gay porn films in the last few years. I started to feel like a star struck kid. Wow! I got fucked by Chuck Wade.

"You are the porn star that is called Chuck Wade, aren't you?" "Yes, that is the name that I use in the porn industry. Have you seen any of my films?" "Hell yes, I use to beat off while watching them. I didn't recognize you at first your hair is a lot longer than in your films." "Yes, when I do a film I have my hair cut down to a military cut. It's an image thing."

"Well Boy, was I as good in person as those films that you saw?" "No comparison man, balling you was the wildest sex that I have ever had. Hell, I will do it with you anytime that you want me too." Brad smiled and laughed a little. He had me and I was to inexperienced to know it.

"How is managing my life connected with making a good

living?" Brad took one of his hands off of the wheel and put it on my leg. He squeezed my leg and said, "Boy, you have talents that you don't know about yet, talents that are in real demand at present."

I acted a little confused. "What talents do you mean?" "Boy have you looked at yourself naked in a mirror lately?" I thought for a moment before I answered. "Yes, I know that I have a good body, it is my only real asset." "Boy, you have a beautiful, almost hairless, natural body. Your skin looks so healthy it glows, your have a really big cock, a great looking ass and best of all, your body reactions while having sex are off the charts. You are a real diamond in the rough and I know exactly how to develop you into star material."

I thought about what Brad had said for a few minutes. Brad just kept driving and left me to think for a while. Finally, I turned to him and said, "You mean that you could make me a star just like you?" "A star yes, but not just like me. I am a major top man in the business. You are more a pretty boy bottom type for now, in short you will get fucked a lot, later you could develop into a major top just like me. That big dick of yours will give you a shot at being a top in the future."

"What about what you said about being your boy?" Brad smiled at me and said, "Boy, I think you are hot and I want you to let me manage you and have you live with me as my boy." "What is a boy?" "Well Boy, in gay life there are four different types of relationships, friends, lovers, boys and slaves. The friend part you already understand. A lover is someone that you love and he is your partner in life. The slave part I never had much use for. A slave is a master's property, not his lover. Slaves are owned property and exist only to serve and please their masters. Frankly, I have known a few slaves in my life and I always thought of them as boring people. Slaves do not interest me. The boy relationship is in between the lover and a slave. A boy belongs to his daddy, but is not owned property. That's why a daddy is sometimes called a daddy master. A boy is his daddy's lover and son. The Daddy is the wiser and more experienced person in the relationship and the boy lets his daddy run his life. The

Boy learns from his Daddy. But, unlike a slave a boy is allowed to have a life and career of his own. Does all of this make any sense to you boy?"

I sat silently for a few minutes. Brad just left me alone. This whole new relationship thing had me confused. I had never had a real relationship and I had never really belonged to anybody or place. In the past few years I had been in a deep closet and I had been basically a loner. The idea of being naked in a movie and having someone make my decisions for me had made me a little uptight. My hands started to shake a little for a few minutes. I am sure that Brad noticed my hands, but he did not say a thing.

After thinking about it I had decided that I could hack the boy thing, god knows I could use an experienced man in my life, but the part about being a porn star I was still not sure about. My hands had now stopped shacking. It was time to ask Brad some more questions.

"Sir, I really like the idea of being your boy, but I don't know if I would be a good porn star." Brad turned to me and said," "Why won't you make a good porn star Boy?" "It is not because I am uptight about doing a nude movie I just don't think that I would look all that good." Brad reaction was unexpected, he started to laugh. "Boy, I know talent when I see it. I know people who are porn stars who don't look half as sexy as you do. I'll tell what I will do, tomorrow just after we get up, we will go downtown and have something to eat and also get you a haircut. Later we will take a hundred or so pictures of you naked in my house and around the pool and the garden and than I will use my movie camera to do a solo test shot of you. Boy, you are going to see that I know what I'm talking about, you have star material. Does that sound good enough for you, Boy?"

"Yes Sir, I would really like to see how the shots come out, because deep down I want to do this, but I have to know if people will laugh at me or not." "Boy, when I'm done with filming you in your first film people are going to come up to you on the street and tell you how much they liked your performance." Brad statement had me feeling better. I could only think, WOW, I was going to be a porn star and get to live with Brad too.

The rest of the way to the beach, Brad and I talked about every subject that popped into our heads, anything from local news to, "Did you see those two hot guys in the blue convertible." We just had a good time, which was a lot of fun, but it did not prepare me for what was to happen at the beach.

When we got Black's Beach I helped Brad unload our beach stuff from the car. I took out beach towels, suntan lotion, food and drinks and sandals. I unpacking everything in the truck I realized that there were no swim trucks. I told Brad this and he started laughing at me. "Boy, this beach is a nude beach you won't need any swim trucks. You are about to get your first lesson in how people will react to seeing you in the nude and get a slight tan in the process."

I didn't complain a bit I just picked up part of the beach stuff and followed Brad down to the nude part of the beach. On the way down to the beach I just thought about what a trip this was going to be. I was actually going to walk around in the nude in front of over a thousand or so strangers. Well, I hope they like me.

Brad seemed to know exactly where he was going and I just tagged behind. Brad stopped in a part of the beach that even I could see had a lot of gay guys. After spreading out the beach towels and stripping off our clothes, Brad handed me some sun tan lotion as we both stood on a beach towel and spread lotion all over our naked bodies. At first I did not pay any real attention to the other people. I was feeling a little uptight at being naked in public. When Brad started to put lotion on my back I looked over the people on the beach and could plainly see that most of them were staring at us. I half smiled back at them.

Brad now told me to put on my sandals and to follow him. As we walked down the beach near the water I could see people, both gay and straight, staring at us and sometimes taking pictures. My problem of being uptight soon pasted as Brad introduced me to several people on the beach, both gay and straight. Several looked me over and made commits such as, "Hey Brad, where did you get the cute stud boy." "Wow, is this your new porn star." And, "Where did you get such a hung, pretty boy." Some of these comments were from straight people. By the time that we left, what the people on the beach had said had me almost convinced that I had a porn star type of body. Well almost, but I still wanted to see the pictures.

A Boner Book

Chapter 3:

THE SHOOT

The next morning Brad woke me up with a hard slap on my bare ass. It seems Brad was an early riser. "Get up Boy it's time to get really for a photo shoot." I got up and sat on the side of the bed and stretched my arms to try to wake up. I looked at my big cock, it was already up and throbbing. It seems my cock was eager to go but that did not stop my hands from shaking. I just sat there for a few minutes and mentally started to relax my body. Finally, my hands stopped shaking and I managed a small smile. Wow, I was going to be a nude model today and maybe change my life for the better

We had cereal and fruit for breakfast out on the patio, near the pool. The idea of being Brad's boy and living in his beautiful house was getting to me. In fact, the whole idea of belonging to Brad really turned me on. You might say at this point the Boy thing was a done deal. I wanted to be part of Brad's life. Hell, I just wanted Brad in a really bad way.

The rest of the day I had no need for clothes, I was nude practically all the time. I posed for photos all over the house, by the pool and even in the garden. Brad was quiet a creative photographer. He thought up angles and setting that were really far out. You could say that I was really getting into it.

After the photo shot we snuggled up in bed and sleep for about an hour before we had lunch. During lunch Brad went over what I was to do in a solo movie shoot. It was to be run as an interview. I was given a list of questions that I would be asked and Brad told me to act natural and give him some interesting answers.

As Brad set up the camera equipment in one of the bedrooms, I studied the list of questions. Most of the questions were basic get to know you questions, but some were more kinky like "What is the strangest place that you have had sex?"

Brad had me put on some walking shorts, polo shirt and some tennis shoes for the shoot. During the shoot I would just sit in a high back chair in the bedroom, talk to Brad about myself and than strip down and slowly beat off. When it came to exactly what I was to do I was a little confused, but Brad said, "Don't worry you can just wing it. You will do all right. I will guide you though it." I was already learning to trust Brad's judgment, after all he was the expert and I began to act eager to get started.

When Brad had the set really he called me into the bedroom. "Boy did you review the questions as I told you too?" "Yes Sir, I know what to say." Brad looked pleased. I was told to sit in the chair and look directly at the camera. Brad than adjusted the lighting and tested some equipment. We were ready to go and best of all hands were not shaking.

Brad sat in a small chair next to the camera and looked at me and smiled, "Well Boy, are you really to begin?" "Yes Sir, I'm ready." Brad started the camera and started to ask me some basic questions. "What is you name and where are you from?" "My name is Jimmy and I grow up in Indiana." "How old are you Jimmy?" "I am 18 years old." "Wow, you are just barely legal." What followed were questions about my boyhood and what I liked about it and what I hated. I don't know why but the idea of being in front of a camera was starting to turn me on, my cock was already half hard and I could feel a surge of sexual energy flowing though my body.

"Well Jimmy, you have had an interesting boyhood. Now let's see what you look like naked." "O.K. so you want me to strip." "Yes, that's the general idea." I took off my tennis shoes and socks first and than my shirt and shorts. When I sat down in the chair again my cock was already hard and throbbing up and down.

"Well Jimmy, I see that you are eager to show off your big piece of meat. How big is your cock?" "It's 9 and one half inches, by 8 inches." "Would you consider your big cock to be your best point?" "No, I have been told that I have a good body and a cute ass." "Can you show us that cute ass of yours?" I did not say a word I just got up and turned around exposing my ass to the camera. "Wow, your do have a cute ass. Could you bend over and give us a better view?" I just followed Brad's instructions and than sat down again.

"Well Jimmy, let's see you stroke your big cock for us." "O.K.", I grabbed a tube of Lube and put a liberal amount on my now throbbing cock and started to slowly beat my meat. "How does that feel Jimmy?" "Wild, it is really starting to turn me on."

After I had stroked my cock for several minutes I had to stop and squeeze the head of my cock really hard. "Well Jimmy you nearly lose your load, didn't you?" I smiled, ear to ear and said, "Yes, I'm very horny today." "I noticed that you had to squeeze the head of your dick to stop from cumming, is that the only way you can do it?" "Yes, once my cock starts to build up to cumming I can't stop it any other way." "You mean that if you stopped beating your meat and didn't touch yourself at all that you would still shoot a big load?" "Yes, that is true. I can't stop from cumming any other way."

"How about showing us what would happen if you didn't squeeze the head of your dick. Let's see you cum without touching yourself." I just smiled at the camera. This was going to be wild. I started to slowly stroke my cock and in only about a minute I was past the point of no return. I let go of my cock and it throb up and down for almost another minute, before my face tensed-up, my body started to shake and my eyes started to roll back until I was looking at the ceiling. My cock just erupted and shot stream after stream of warn, sticky cum several feet into the air, as my body violently shook. When my cock was spent and my body relaxed I looked into the camera and smiled.

With cum dripping off of my face and running down my naked body, Brad continued to ask me questions. "Wow, that was some show, I have never seen anyone cum like that before. How many times can you cum in one day?" "If I wanted to I could get off 10 times a day." "How many times do you cum per day on average?" "While I can cum again and again, every day, I don't need to. I can get by with once a month if I have too."

"Unlike most young men you seem to be able to control your cock, rather than the other way around. What is your biggest sexual fantasy?" "I would have to say that my biggest fantasy is to live with a major gay porn star. That would really turn me on." Brad just smiled, I was his and he knew it.

After the shot I headed for the shower while Brad put away the equipment. After I finished showering Brad told me to relax for a while and to not get dressed. It seemed Brad liked to see me naked and he was getting more bossy. At first it startled me a little, the fact that Brad was starting to take over my life, but I quickly got use to his ways. I even started to like being bossed by Brad.

When Brad was done developing the film from the shot he called me into the camera equipment room to view the slides of the photo shot. As we went over the over two hundred color slides Brad picked out the ones he thought were the best shots. He picked out about 20 slides and put them on the bottom of the light board for me to look at.

I had to admit, I looked good, as good as most porn photos that I had seen, maybe better than most. Brad acted pleased with his work.

His talent for taking nude photos had really paid off. I had to admit that Brad was right I was a porn quality young man and I was soon to find out that Brad was always right. It wasn't just his ego he was just good at what he does.

Reviewing the solo movie of myself was more interesting, it was more like a real porn movie and I could see exactly how I came across on film. Brad put the tape in the VCR and had me sit naked at his feet, while he sat in a living room chair. He raped his legs around me as we both watched the tape of my little solo performance.

As we watched the film every once and a while Brad would bend over and run his hands down my naked body and play with my cock and balls. I took this as a compliment. I liked it when Brad paid attention to me. The lust I thought that I saw in Brad's eyes would, I'm sorry to say, turn out to be dollar sights. With all the experience that Brad had in the porn business he knew that his new boy was worth a lot of money. But at the time I was young and rather dumb about the ways of the world. I just wanted to be part of Brad's life.

The solo film of me jerking off convinced me that I could make gay porn films and that people would like what they saw. After the movie ended Brad took the tape out of the machine and turned to look at me sitting naked on the floor. "Well Boy, I don't know about you but I think you were great. What do you think of your performance?" "I liked it and I have decided to make some porn films." "Does that mean that you want to be my boy too?" "Yes Sir, it does. I want to belong to you." "Do you mean that I am the boss?" "Yes Sir, you are the boss." Brad smiled, he had me and I was his new little money maker.

Brad put away the tape and than took off his clothes. His cock was already hard. I smiled, I was going to get some action. Brad walked over to me and told me to get up. "Yes Sir!" He grabbed the hair on the back of my head, tilted my head back and kissed me as he played with my now hard cock and fondled my balls.

"Well Boy, you did so well today that I have decided to reward you, I am going to take you into the bedroom and royally fuck my new boy. Follow me Boy." "Yes Sir!" and for the next few hours Brad ravaged my naked body like a hungry animal. It was some of the best sex of my young life. I was in love with Brad. But, Brad I doubt was in love with me, he was more likely just claiming his new property. Brad was the professional L.A. hustler who was just keeping his new little money maker happy and he was damn good at it. I was in love and it would be some time before I realized who the real Brad was.

I quickly got use to Brad's dominating ways and I settled into a servant type of life style. Brad was the boss and I did what he said. I signed a three year contract with his film company. I was going to be a gay porn star.

About two weeks after I had moved in with Brad and let him take over my life, my film career started. Early one Monday morning Brad got me out of bed early. Once I was on my feet Brad gave me a big hug. He than backed away from me and visually inspected my aroused naked body. My cock was throbbing hard. I had not been allowed to cum in over a week, Brad's orders. Brad stared into my half awake eyes and said, "Well Boy, today you are going to become a star." "Yes Sir, I'll do my best to make you proud of me."

My reply seemed to please my Daddy. His boy was ready to perform for him. "O.K. Boy, fix us a light breakfast and don't get dressed till I tell you to, "Yes Sir." My Daddy like to see me working around the house in the nude, so that he could fondle me and play with my cute ass anytime that he wished. As for me, I enjoy the attention. It makes me feel needed, which is a feeling that I seldom got back home in Indiana and it keeps my dick hard. Being turned on seems to give me more energy and attract more attention from my daddy. Both of which are good things in my book.

The location for the shoot was at a private home in the Hollywood Hills. When we got the address Brad pulled off the road into tree lined drive way that led to an iron gate. Brad honked the car horn twice and the gate started to open. Inside the gate was a small parking lot that was big enough for only 4 cars.

As the car came to a halt, Brad turned to me and smiled, "O.K Boy lets go." He had that gleam in his eyes that I was starting to believed meant that he was proud of me.

As we approached the house I could see that it was a simple one story building with a pool in the backyard. The owner of the house came out to meet us. Brad introduced us, "Jimmy I would like you to meet Mr. Johnston." Mr. Johnston was a stocky man with a short, well-trimmed beard. I figured him to be about in his 60's. I stepped forward and shook his hand. "It's nice to meet you Mr. Johnston." The man smiled, "It's good to meet you too. You can just call me Jesse, everyone else does."

Mr. Johnston than turned to look at Brad, "Well Brad is this sexy young man your new porn star?" Brad managed a slight smile. "If you think he is sexy now Jesse just wait until you see him buck naked. He will really blow your socks off." Mr. Johnston started to laugh a little. "Hell, at my age such a welcomed sight could be more of a health risk than a turn-on. But I'm more than willing to take the risk."

We both followed Mr. Johnston into his house and he told us to make ourselves comfortable in the living room. As we sat down on a large leather sofa two more men entered the room. "Hi Brad." "Well, it is good to see that you two found the house without any trouble." "Hey, have faith man." The second man than cut in, "It was easy finding Jesse's place, we have both been here many times for some of Jesse's famous dinner parties and we have helped film several porn flicks here too."

Brad now turned to me and said, "Jimmy I would like you to meet Noll and Rick, two of the best camera men in the porn business." I smiled and shook hands with the both of them. Both of the camera men smiled at me as if they were undressing me. I blushed a little. Back home in Indiana I seldom got such attention, except in the school shower room and never when I was looking directly at the person. Being some sort of sex object was a new feeling to me. The whole scene made me a little nervous.

Brad quickly took command. "Well Noll, are you and Rick ready to roll?" "Yes, the cameras are loaded and we have read the script" "O.K. get the cameras and we will start work on the first scene." With that Brad, myself and the camera guys left the house and piled into two cars and headed down the street to we came to an isolated road with very few houses on it. The first scene was a simple shoot. In this scene I was a hitch hiker and Brad stopped, talked to me in a sexy lets fuck voice and I smiled and got into the car.

Back at the house the second scene was the sex scene. After the camera men filmed us going into the house they switched positions and filmed us coming though the front door. Brad than turned to me and said, "Well Jimmy go into the living and take off your clothes. I will get us some wine and be back in a minute." It was in the script, but it was not original material. Brad had written our first meeting into my first film. At the time I felt pleased that Brad wanted to record a lasting memory of our first day in his house.

As Brad left the room the two camera men changed positions and worked on the camera positions and lighting. When they were ready, they filmed me slowing taking off my clothes and looking a little nervous and confused, just like it had happened. When I was totally naked, with a roaring hard-on, the camera men said cut and I was left a standing naked in the middle of the room as they rearranged everything again, in order to film Brad coming back into the room.

The scenes that followed were all right out of Brad and my personal history, almost word for word, scene for scene. It was like reliving that first day with Brad. Brad had written our own little living history for the whole world to see. Well, may be just the porn buying gay part.

My first acting job as a gay porn star was interesting, but a little unnerving. Even time I really got into a scene someone was yelling cut and we had to wait until the crew made some adjustments, or took a series of still photographs. Sometimes these breaks could last a half hour at a time. Mr. Johnston was nice enough to lend Brad and me some bath robes to wear between shoots.

Other problems that I had to get used to were the heat and sometimes blinding glare from the lights, keeping my dick hard when needed and putting up with the two camera men, who had a bad habit of grabbing a quick feel when ever they could. During one break in the shooting Noll offered to pay me $300 dollars for a chance to suck me off and fuck me after the shoot was over. I just smiled and walked away. Brad didn't seem to notice, he was almost always busy reviewing the film that we just shoot. After a while I got the impression that this was normal behavior in the business. I got used to avoiding the camera men as much as possible. My ass, cock and balls got a real good workout that day and not just from having sex with Brad.

It must say that Mr. Johnston was a really gentlemen that day. He just sat in the background and watched the show. Afterward, Mr. Johnston prepared a great dinner for the crew and served it out next to the pool. Eating a tasty dinner and looking into Brad's eyes, as the sun went down, made me almost forget what a strange day it had been.

On the way home Brad went over my performance. "Boy, you did very well for your first time under the lights. You had very few real problems and you put one great performance. I was really proud of the way you were always able to get it up when ever the scene required a stiff one. I especially liked the way you were able to keep a roaring hard-on when I royally fucked you for a long period of time. I hate to see a guy getting fucked in a porn film with a soft dick. It tells the whole audience that he doesn't really enjoy getting a stiff one up the ass. You really enjoy getting fucked and it will show up on film, I just know it will." I thanked Brad for his compliment. I liked pleasing Brad, even if it meant having camera men play with my ass and cock.

I started to feel better about my performance that day. I had pleased Brad and it also made me feel like I was now paying my own way in the world. The feel and warmth of Brad's naked body that night had me feeling relax in no time and I quickly fell asleep.

It took Brad and his crew a month to shoot the three extra scenes needed to finish the movie. I was allowed to help with the production of the others parts of the movie. Even with clothes on the camera men still played with my ass and groped me. They also started to call me sweet cheeks.

After seeing the other actors, several very muscular, young guys, I started to worry a little worried. Would I look good in comparison to these muscle bound guys? I had more of a basic muscular swimmers body.

When Brad was finished filming, cutting and packaging the film it was quickly put on the market. Brad titled the movie, First Meetings. He was right about the film making me a star. Within 3 months of its release we knew it was a big hit and people started to recognize me in public. Fan letters and e-mails gave Brad the impression that I was the big attraction of the film. Brad started to make plans for putting me into more movies.

So began my gay porn career. I was now, so to speak, in the public eye and Brad started to give me lessons in social skills, like how to talk to fans and even how to dress. Since I am basically a shy person, this star thing made me nervous. I never really got used to being the center of attention.

Financially, I did not see much of the success that my career was having. I was put on an allowance of only $1,000 a month and given a new Jetta to run around in. My duties were to keep house for Brad, make porn movies and to be Brad's boy.

After about 6 months my duties were increased. I now was a very popular new gay porn star. I was recognized when ever Brad took me to a gay part of town, so Brad decided to cash in on my success even more. Brad announced to me, "Boy it's time for you to start to make some real money. The movies don't pay very well, so you will be working for my escort service from the rest of your contract. I already have 70 clients lined up who want to hire you." My contract was for 3 years, so it looked like I was going to be a professional whore for the next 2 and one half years. At first the idea had me sitting on the floor of my daddy's bedroom and shaking. I don't know if I could hack this new job and I was afraid at first of being busted by the police. But, Brad went over his method of business with me. It seems his boys only service a select list of clients, about 300 people and the chances of trouble with the police is very small. In fact, none of his boys has ever had a problem. Brad soon convinced me that as usual he knew what he was doing. So I became a high priced hustler.

I quickly adjusted to being a male whore. I found that I had a talent for it. Maybe, it was the pay. I was marketed at first for $500 an hour and there were a steady stream of eager customers. I had two to three customers a day and I only took one day off a week

The money, of course, was handled by my Daddy. I was allowed to keep the tips and my allowance was raised to $2000 a month. I sensed that I was not being treated fairly, but I loved Brad and I never said a word. I just banked my allowance and most of the tips and tried to pay no attention to what Brad was doing with the rest. The only mention that Brad ever made to the rest of what I earned was that he had invested it for us.

Not that I hated being a high paid male whore, I actually really got into it. I found I liked pleasing older men sexually and emotionally. Brad told me that it would not be a hard job and he was right. He told me, "Boy, you are going to find out that the higher the price the hustler charges the less he actually has to do." He was right again most of my clients were easy to satisfy sexually. Most of them were highly educated and wealthy professionals and they seem to be more interested in meeting and talking to me than in sex. Most of the time I just got a blow job or they wanted to fuck me. Fucking, hell I love to be fucked. So the whole job wanted as hard as I at first thought.

Some of the assignments were actually fun, like the times I was a stripper for a party, or a nude waiter for a private event. I not only had fun, the tips were very good at these events.

I was proud of myself in a way. I had adjusted well to my new life. I had a dream of a lover, who actually treated very well at home at least and I lived very well. Did a poor boy from Indiana, like me, really have a reason to complain? Well, in my own little dream world that is what I believed. Brad knew what was best for me and that was that.

My little dream world started to change after I had lived with Brad for a year and a half. Brad was a very business minded man and I guess that he saw what he had been able to accomplish with me and decided to expand his business. Soon, two more boys were recruited to make films, work for Brad's escort service and live in his house with us. It got so that I seldom got to sleep with or have sex with my Daddy. Even star struck boy like me could see that it was not working out any more and after two years of living with my Daddy I decided to leave and do what I had wanted to do since I was very young.

Chapter 4:

PARIS

I had dreamed for years about taking a vacation to Europe. But, since my teenage years and living situations were far from good, it was just a dream. As a teenager in a small town in Indiana I never had much money to call my own. Hell, it was a struggle just to have enough to eat and basic things like clothes. So saving money for a dream vacation was like wishing for the stars.

Since my parents had died when I was just 10 years old, I had become a ward of the state. Until I graduated from high school I lived in foster and group homes. During these years there was never enough of anything. I wore hand me down clothes and just hoped that the food served at meal times was worth eating. The idea of having a car, like other teenagers, was out of the question. Hell, I didn't even have a bike.

But, I survived my less than ideal childhood, graduated with honors from high school, managed to not use drugs and stayed out of trouble with the law. Maybe, I survived because of my dreams about getting out of that small town, or possibly because I always knew that

I had a reason for existing in this life. What event that meant.

Now that I had finally had the courage and common sense to leave Brad and follow my dream, my spirits were high once again. I was going to find out what Europe and especially Paris were like and maybe find out why the city of Paris had always fascinated me, like it was part of my future destiny, or something.

Money was no longer a barrier, as it was when I was a teenager. I had been ripped off financially by Brad for a lot of money, but I had saved almost all of my allowances and most of my tip money. It added up to enough money to enable me to live in Europe for a year or two if I wanted too. Without having to really worry about money for the first time in my life I was looking forward to what ever was waiting for me in Europe.

After flying into Paris, I took a cab to a small tourist hotel that I had booked in advance. I picked this hotel because it was cheap and it was near the gay leather bars in the city. My relationship with Brad had not worked out, but I still liked dominate men. Dominate men who are successful, intelligent and in control of their lives really turn me on. Maybe, I could find such a man in one of the gay leather bars in Paris. If not Paris, possibly some other part of Europe, I had to give it a try.

Just after arriving at my hotel and unpacking I slept for a few hours to get rid of the sense of jet lag I had developed. I guess that I don't travel to well. By the time that I woke up it was early evening and I was hungry. I asked the man at the hotel desk about the location of a good café and he was very helpful.

The café that I picked had very good food and sitting at an outdoor table gave me a good view of the local people and the tourists who were walking through the area. I could not help but notice how good looking some of the men on the street were, as I inspected every inch of any good looking man that came down the street.

After about a half hour of eyeballing the men on the street I saw one young man who just stood out from the crowd. He was a dark haired, well-built young man that looked like he was in his late 20's. As he past the café I caught his eye and he smiled, but continued to walk down the street. I don't know what it was about him, there were other men on the street that night that were just as good-looking, he just had something and he turned me on to no end. As the young man of my dreams disappeared into the crowd I let out a small moan.

The young man was gone and why I was so attracted to him was a mystery. After finishing my meal I headed back to my hotel room, to get ready to go out to the local leather bars.

I had packed very little, only some basic come fuck me type clothes for cruising the bars and some practical street clothes. I laid out my bar cruising clothes, two pairs of old jeans, several tea shirts and a pair of tennis shoes. If Brad had taught me anything it was that I was a daddy's boy and it was a role that I was comfortable in playing, so I had only packed boy clothes, so to speak.

I stripped off my clothes and looked at myself naked in the full length mirror on the back of the closet door. I knew that I had been a big success as a porn star in America, but would I be attractive to European men? The image in the mirror was of a young man, who was 5'10" tall and had a muscular, smooth bodied, swimmers build. As usual what really stood out in the mirror image was my big 9 and one half inch cock.

I didn't know if this combination would sell in Paris, but I did know that I wanted to have a man. Hell, I needed to get fucked so bad that my cock was already hard and throbbing just thinking about it. Suddenly, I started to think about my present situation. I had a good body, no real money worries and I was healthy. The only problem was that I had no man and no home. I knew from past experience that I don't function very well alone. If being with Brad taught me anything useful it was that dominating and successful men make me feel safe and secure. My thoughts had an effect on my body, my hands started to shake again.

I sat down naked, with my back against the wall and rapped my arms around my folded legs. I thought to myself that everything will be alright and that I would find a new man and have a home again. After about 10 minutes my hands stopped shaking and I started to get dress to cruise the leather bars.

The first bar that I visited did not pan out, no hot leather men. The only interesting action that I got was when several patrons recognized me from the film work that I had done with Brad's company. My fans bought me a beer and we talked for a while. The hour that I spent in that bar was not a waste of time, my fans were very nice and they told me which bar the hot, young leather men go to. So after hugging my fans I headed for the bar that they had told me about.

The crowd at the next bar was younger and better looking. I could feel the vibrations in the air the first minute that I stepped into the bar. My sexual energy just started to rise as I walked over to the bar and ordered a beer. After leaning up against a wall and surveying the crowd I quickly realized that if I wanted to find a dominating gay male in Paris this was the place to be.

As I slowly sipped my beer I looked over the crowd. I spotted several men that looked promising, but one young man just stood out of the crowd. At first, I could only see him from the back. He was dark haired and he was wearing a leather coat, tight fitting old jeans and boots. I couldn't help but notice how well his butt filled out his tight jeans. I was so horny that I felt like going over to him and grabbing his pretty ass right than an there. This young man was having quiet an effect on me, but I was not prepared for what was to come.

All of a sudden, the young man that I lusted after turned around. I felt a little light headed as my eyes caught his and he smiled at me. He was the same man I had seen on the street when I was having dinner. I smiled back at him and he walked over to me and introduced himself. "Hello, my name is Carlos what is your name?" I caught my breath and said, "My name is James, people just call me Jimmy." Carlos smiled and looked deep into my eyes. "Well, Jimmy it is pleasure to meet you. You are an American, is that right?" "Yes, I'm from California." "I see that California has some very good looking young men. I will have to visit in the near future. You must tell me about yourself and California." "O.K., I would like to talk to you more." "Let's find a quiet place in the back were we can talk." Carlos motioned for me to follow him and he led me to an area of the bar that had very few people. We both sat down at a small table and I found myself gazing into his eyes from across the table. Carlos smiled and grabbed both of my hands and held them tight.

We talked about each other and California for the next two hours. Carlos had my full attention the whole time. I was fascinated by his looks and the way he handled himself. Carlos was not only good looking and had a great body, but he was also well educated and he could talk about almost any subject. He said that he was French/Moroccan by birth, but he had been educated in France and England. Even with my Brad experience still fresh in my mind Carlos soon had me literally eating out of his hand. I told him all about my childhood in Indiana and my boy training with Brad. The boy thing fascinated Carlos, it seems he had trained two daddy's boys of his own in the past and he really missed not having a boy in his life. By the time he asked me to go home with him Carlos had me in his pocket. I was going to be Carlos's boy for the night. How could I say no, Carlos was just the type of dominate gay man that really turned me on.

Carlos had parked his car only a block away from the bar. I was a little surprised to find that Carlos drove a new Mercedes sedan. It was the expensive model. You know, the one kids call a Big Ass Mercedes. It seems there was more to Carlos than just a pretty face and great body.

Carlos lived in a house that to me looked like a townhouse. It was three stories high and located in an expensive area of Paris. I was new to the city and I had not idea where I was. Carlos parked his car in the garage. As we got out of the car a surge of sexual energy ran threw my body, making my cock hard as a rock. Carlos unlocked the door to the house and motioned for me to follow him.

As we entered the kitchen Carlos turned around, looked into

my eyes and half smiled. He than walked forward, grabbed me by the cock and laid a big wet kiss on my lips. My body squirmed. As he moved his lips away from mine he looked me over and said, "You are a very pretty young man and I want to start to train you in how to please me." He than ordered me to take off my clothes. As I unzipped my jeans and slid them off, Carlos started to smile. He liked what he saw.

Carlos told me to follow him upstairs to his bedroom. As I walked naked though several expensively decorated rooms of Carlos's house, my rock hard cock throbbed up and down. Jolts of sexual energy pulsated thought out my body. Following Carlos up the stairs and watching his beautiful rounded ass move around in his tight jeans was starting to drive my cock crazy.

As we entered Carlos's bedroom, I was told to get on my knees. As I knelt on the bedroom floor, Carlos slowly took off his leather vest and than his shirt, exposing a very muscular, semi-hairy chest. He than sat down in a chair, next to the bed, unzipped his jeans and took out about 8 inches of hard cock. He looked at me and said, "Boy, come over and eat me and than suck your daddy's cock." "Yes Sir!" I didn't need any more encouragement. I was so horny that beads of pre-cum were starting to run down the length of my pulsating cock.

I walked over to the chair, knelt down and slowly started to lick my daddy's balls, from one side to the other. Carlos started to moan and he flexed his legs. He liked what I was doing. I than ran my tongue up his wildly throbbing cock, licked around the bouncing head several times, just before I swallowed his cock down to his hair. He moaned and said, "Good Boy, suck it, suck it good." The feel of having me deep throat his cock again and again soon had him moaning louder and louder, until after several minutes, he could not hold back any longer. Just as he was about to cum, he forced my head down on his cock and shot a big load down my throat. My head felt light and my heart pounded faster and faster, as Carlos's cock repeatedly swelled, as it pumped stream after stream of warm, sweet cum down my eager throat.

As Carlos continued to moan and his body squirmed, I licked the last drops of sweet cum off of his cock, before I started to play with the head of his still hard and throbbing cock with my tongue. Carlos moaned and his body shook as he said, "God Boy, you are really good at sucking cock." He than leaned forward, grabbed me by the hair and pulled my head back, before he began to give me a deep, long kiss that almost had me shoot my load.

As his tongue probed deep into my mouth, I could feel his hands playing with my ass. Just as Carlos started to massage my ass cheeks with his fingers and play with my asshole, I started to breath faster and faster, as I quietly said, "Please Daddy, fuck me Daddy, please fuck me."

Carlos withdrew his hand from my ass and stood up and than he slowly stripped off the rest of his clothes, until he was standing in front of me totally naked with a throbbing hard cock and a very animalistic, hungry look in his eyes. He than walked around in back of me, put his hands under my armpits and lifted me up on to my feet, just before he started to kiss and lick the back of my neck, than my shoulders and finally he tongued his way down to my ass. He now spread my ass cheeks and started to give me the best rimming that I have had in years. He was so good I had to pinch the head of my throbbing cock, in order to keep from cumming all over the bedroom rug.

As my body relaxed, Carlos licked and kissed his way up my back, before he started to kiss the sides of my neck, as his cock throbbed up and down on my ass, causing me to squirm and sexually yearn to be fucked. Just as Carlos started to lightly nibble on my ear lobes his hand slid down to my bare ass and his fingers started to play with my asshole, causing me to shake and loudly moan.

I moaned and said, "Oh god, oh that feels so good," as I felt a wet finger start to probe the inside of my ass. First one finger, than two and finally three fingers massaged the interior of my ass, causing me to moan and squirm so violently that I almost lost my load.

I continued to squirm, with every movement of his fingers. Suddenly Carlos withdrew his fingers and my body began to relax. He gently moved me forward and positioned me face down on the bed and I soon felt the sensation of a greased cock slide deep into my ass. I yelled and my body shook as I slowly got used to the heavenly feel of a man's cock inside of me once again.

Carlos did not let up, he repeatedly rammed his cock deep into me, as I moaned and my body shook. The more that I moaned and squirmed, the more Carlos shoved it to me. What he saw as my pain only seemed to turn him on, more and more, as his cock seemed to get harder with each violent thrust.

But, the pain that Carlos was inflecting on me was not really hurting me. It was only causing my body to rapidly build up to a violent climax. As both I and Carlos got closer to cumming, he turned me over on my back and started to thrust his cock into me faster and faster, just as he reached forward and grabbed my nibbles and started to squeeze them really hard. I started to loudly moan and my body started to violently shake, as I got closer and closer to cumming Carlos's body tensed up and he started to grit his teeth. I was about to cum and I began to moan so loud that I almost screamed. Carlos shot a big load up my ass that caused me to unload stream after stream of warm cum all over my upper body.

After Carlos withdrew he leaned forward, sweat was dripping off his body on to mine as he looked into my eyes and smiled. "That was the wildest fuck I have ever had. Yank, you are really great sex." With that, Carlos reached under the bed to get a towel. He cleaned my cum off of me and than led me into the bathroom for a nice warm shower. As we both got into bed, Carlos gave me a kiss and than he laid down beside me. I rolled over, leaned up against his naked body and put my head on his chest. Both of his arms moved over my back and without another word we both relaxed and drifted off to sleep.

I woke up to the feel of Carlos massaging my back. I looked

up and smiled. "Well Boy that was a great show that you put on last night. It was so good I want to ask you to spend the next week with me. You not only turn me on, you are the most fascinating boy that I have ever met and I want to find out a lot more about you.

I wanted to belong to this beautiful young stud and I eagerly agreed to spend the next week doing everything that I could to make Carlos believe that he had to make me his boy. It was a week long labor of pleasure and Carlos asked for the right to train me to be his boy and be part of his life. I agreed. I now felt needed and safe, I had a man and a home once again.

Chapter 5:

CARLOS'S RELATIVES

The next six months were both challenging and exciting. Carlos trained me in how to serve and please my new daddy master. The training at times was hard. While Carlos was more affectionate and attentive than Brad, he was also a much stricter task master.

Carlos seemed very pleased with how I had adjusted to living with him as his new boy. I had quickly learned what was expected of me and I settled into the routine of caring for Carlos and running his house. Unlike my life as Brad's boy, Carlos did not want me to work outside of the house. I was his boy and he wanted me to just focus on serving him and not be concern myself with what is happening in the out side world. My new life of just caring for my daddy and his home suited me just find. I was very content with my new life and I became completely devoted to pleasing Carlos.

I was happy, when Carlos said that we were going to Morocco to see his family. This only made me feel like I was now a real part of Carlos's life. I didn't suspect in the least that this trip would radically change my life. The next day, we boarded a plane, for a quick flight to Morocco.

Carlos's father Omar picked us up at the airport. The family home was about an hours drive outside the Moroccan city of Casablanca. Carlos's family home was in a walled compound, near the sea. Carlos and I were warmly greeted by his two older brothers, Omar Jr. and Pierre. Omar Jr. was Carlos's older brother. He was also dark haired and well built, but he was not as good looking as Carlos. Omar Jr. was also a fairly shy person. He tended to let his father do the talking. Pierre was the shortest of the brothers and the youngest. He was the only family member to have light hair. He was a red head. Unlike his oldest brother he had a very out going personality and he loved to talk. Carlos had no sisters, his mother was dead and his brothers had not married. So, Carlos family was made up of only men.

For the first few hours that we were at the family compound Carlos showed me around his boyhood home and the beach near the house. We ended up watching the sun set on the beach before we headed back to have dinner with Carlos's family.

The main dish for dinner was lamb and the dinner conversation centered around Carlos's boyhood. The family seemed to thing that Carlos was the family golden boy and that he could do no wrong.

The next day after breakfast, Carlos and I decided to drive into the local town and do some shopping in the local outdoor market. We intended to just buy some local foods and vegetables, for that night's dinner. While walking down an alley, next to the market, a van suddenly pulled up in front of us and three hooded men burst out, knocked me aside and grabbed Carlos. Carlos yelled at me to run and I did as he said. I ran down the alley to the street and tried to get help, but I did not know any of the local languages and I couldn't make myself understood. In frustration I walked back to the alley. Carlos and the van were gone. My heart sank and I sat down on an old wooden shipping crate and tried to figure out what I was to do next.

I decided the only thing that I could do was to drive back to the family compound and tell Carlos's family what had happen. The news that Carlos had been kidnapped by some several hooded men caused a panic in the family. I didn't know what I could do to help out. I just sat down and watched the family make frantic phone calls and talk in languages that I did not understand. But, it was apparent, even to me, that they were trying to find out what had really happened to Carlos.

After several hours had pasted, Carlos's father Omar, told us what had happened. "The Hussiens have taken Carlos." Carlos's two brothers than asked, "Well, what do they want for him?" It seemed that Carlos had been kidnapped by enemies of the family and the kidnappers wanted a ransom

The kidnappers wanted $200,000 in American dollars, or something that was worth the same or more. Carlos's dad put his hands on his face and started to cry. "We don't have what they want."

I asked what will happen to Carlos if the ransom is not paid. Pierre just shook his head and said, "They will torture Carlos and than kill him. We won't even have a body to bury." Pierre went on to say that the Hussiens are blood enemies of his family. They were a bunch of murdering thieves. He hated them.

I was eager to be of some help and I asked, "I understand the part about $200,000 in American dollar, but what do they mean by something worth the same amount or more?" Pierre and Omar Jr. just stared at me for a moment. Their eyes lit up as if they had an idea. "Well James, the other part means something that they can sell for at least $200,000, such as gold, land, drugs and slaves."

I understood what they meant except the part about the slaves. "What do you mean slaves, wasn't slavery outlawed a long time ago?" Pierre and Omar Jr. just nodded in agreement. "Yes that is true in most cases, but not in the special market that the Hussiens deal in. It is not the old fashion type of slavery. It is a special type. It is a market in good looking young male slaves, who are sold to a wealthy master for a period of five years."

The whole thing was still a little confusing to me. Slavery in this day and age, it doesn't seem possible. But, as Pierre continued to example, I realized that I was wrong, a special market in young male slaves did exist. It sold only young, good-looking males, who volunteered to be sold and the slaves got half of the sale price in a trust for them and their master got the other half. A good-looking, well-trained male slave could sell for several hundred thousand dollars. Carlos had been sold for over four hundred thousand dollars.

I was greatly surprised to learn that Carlos had once been sold into slavery for five years when he was just 18 years old. It seems his father had been taken prisoner by the Hussiens after a gun battle between the families and Carlos had volunteered to be trained and sold as the ransom. Carlos had been intensively trained for six months by a professional military man, who was hired by the Hussiens and than sold at a special auction in order to get Omar Sr. back alive. Carlos became a rich German master's property for five year. In sort, he was a wealthy man's sex toy for five years. This is a fact that Carlos had never mentioned to me.

This arrangement has become a sometimes used method of operation for both families, basically because both sides end up winners in some way. The kidnappers get their ransom and the kidnapped person is set free. The slave gets a large chuck of money in trust to use after his period of slavery. This arrangement is how this secret slave market is kept alive.

As Pierre continued the tale I was soon to learn that Carlos's family were not just victims, they had done the same thing to the Hussiens after Carlos was free again. That time the Hussiens gave up a good-looking male cousin, who was only 16 years old at the time. He was sold to a rich master from South America for five years.

It seemed the Hussiens were only getting back at Carlos's family for what they had done 5 years ago. This time Carlos's family had a problem they had no more family members that were good-looking enough, or young enough to satisfy the standards of this special slave market. It was at this point that I started to feel very uneasy, since both of Carlos brothers and his father were now staring at me. My hands began to shake.

The way that Carlos family was looking at me made it obvious, they wanted me to volunteer to be trained and sold as a master's slave for five years. But, the whole idea really scared me and I just remained silent, as my hands continued to shake.

Nothing much was said, I was left to my own thoughts for the next few hours, as Carlos's family make numerous phone calls. After each phone call Carlos's brothers looked more and more frustrated. Finally, Pierre and Omar Sr. sat down next to me on the living room sofa and bluntly told me that I had to volunteer, it was the only way to save Carlos.

The whole idea scared the hell out of me and I told them I had to think about it for a while. My instincts were telling me to say no, even to get the hell out of there, but my love for Carlos kept me thinking about doing it. I knew that I could hack it, I could be a slave and a good one, but I did not like the whole idea of being enslaved, even if I would end up with some real money in the end. I was a daddy's boy, which is half way to being a slave, but I had a mental block that stopped me from crossing the line into total slavery.

The next day, a policeman came to visit the family. He was one of Carlos's uncles. Carlos's two brothers talked to him on the street in front of the family compound. As I watched the men talk, I was getting a bad feeling about the whole issue, like I was being pushed in a direction that I did not want to go. My feelings would turn out to be right.

After about an hour of talking to the policeman, Carlos's brothers came back to the house and told me that the policeman wanted to discuss something with me. I knew right than and there that my decision had already been made for me.

When I walked outside to meet the policeman, he greeted

me in a rather cold fashion. He said, "I am here as a friend of the family, not a policeman. So, what I have to say is personal, not police business. Carlos's brother's told me that he has explained the situation to you. The only way this family has of saving Carlos's life is to give the kidnappers what they want. The family has very little money at present. They live comfortably, but they are not rich. That only leaves one possible solution to this situation and it concerns you." "Yes, I know what you are going to say, that I should offer myself to be trained and sold as a slave for the next five years. But, the idea scares me. I just can't do it."

The policeman gave me a cold stare. He did not say a word he just started to walk around me as if he were inspecting me. Suddenly, in a forceful manner, the policeman said, "Boy, take off your clothes, I want to have a good look at your body." I don't know why, but I just started to undress. When I was completely naked the policeman visually inspected my naked body and than said, "Boy, you are a very pretty and well-built young man. If the Hussiens see you naked, I am sure that they will trade Carlos for the chance to train and sell you at auction."

I could not look at the policeman I just bowed my head and looked at the ground. He walked over and stood in front of me and grabbed my chin and lifted my head up, until he was looking directly into my eyes. "What are you afraid of, you will end up being a wealthy man's sex toy for five years and Carlos will still be alive. After five years, you and Carlos can get back together again. Boy, if Carlos could handle being a slave so can you."

I think that the policeman could see by the look on my face that I still was not sold on the idea. I said nothing and just looked at the ground for a few minutes. Suddenly, the policeman seemed to lose his patience with me, he stepped for ward and grabbed me by the balls and started to squeeze. I moaned really loud and my body shook. The policeman looked directly into my startled eyes and said, "Son lets make this decision easy for you. If you decide not to do the honorable thing and volunteer to be sold, I will see to it that you spend the next

20 years in a filthy jail cell." Shocked, I just said, "But, I didn't do anything." "Yes you did, you were responsible for the death of Carlos, who is my favorite nephew. But that is not what the charge will be. I'm a captain of police. I will put a heavy charge on you and make it stick." He now squeezed my balls really hard, causing my body to tense up.

The choice was easy, I agreed to be sold and the policeman released my balls. As I relaxed and started to get dressed I could see that the policeman was smiling. "I knew Boy, that you were a good and honorable young man."

After I had gotten dressed I followed the police captain into the family compound and I told Carlos father that I would volunteer. The family was over joyed. They all hugged me and kissed me on the cheeks. It was not the decision that I wanted to make, but I guess that it was the right one. I felt like a weight had been lifted off of my chest, but I was still scared.

Chapter 6:

GETTING READY

After my announcement, Carlos's father quickly made several phone calls, in an effort to arrange a deal. As Carlos's father talked on the phone I was told by Pierre to just relax, things are being handled. While we waited for news Pierre and Omar Jr. fixed some food for dinner.

About 3 hours later we received word that a possible trade had been arranged, at a desert oasis, about an hours drive from the family home. If the Hussiens liked me, they would give back Carlos after I was trained and sold. I was told to get ready, that I would be driven to the meeting in one hour.

I grabbed my overnight bag and headed for the bathroom, to take a shower and get my mind focused on what I was about to do. As I shaved off, what few whiskers that I had on my boyish face, Pierre turned on the shower water and bought me a pair of sandals and a light cotton robe that opened in the front. I was told that this is what I will wear to the meeting.

After I had stripped naked, I looked at myself in the mirror. Did I have a body that the Hussiens would think is worth $200,000? People have told me that I am a very pretty young man. I have a good looking, smooth skinned, swimmers body, a nice rounded ass and a big dick. Would my porn star/hustler body be enough to make a deal. I can draw a lot of attention on a nude beach or in a gay bathhouse, but is that the type of body that the slavers are interested in? I was used to selling my body for $500 an hour, but I had no idea what someone would pay in order to own me for several years. Well, I can only let them look me over and hope that they are impressed at what they see.

To help my appearance a little, I decided to trim my public and arm pit hair, back to about a quarter of an inch. This gave my body a neat appearance and it made my big dick look a little bigger. My 9 and one half dick now looked more like 10 inches. Pierre now opened the bathroom door and froze. He looked a little startled. "Wow, you are a pretty boy. If the Hussiens don't like you they are crazy." Pierre handed me my robe and told me to quickly get ready to leave. After Pierre left I took one more look at myself in the mirror and for the first time in years I thought about my late parents. My body was the only material thing of value that they had left me. Now I was about to sell it. For a few short minutes I looked at myself in the mirror, as I enjoyed stroking my big, half hard cock a few times. This was probably the last time for next few years that I would be able to play with my own cock with out having to have my master's permission. After tonight my master will own me and he will decide if I can use my cock, if at all. I looked at myself in the mirror one last time and gave my cock one more stroke, before I let go of my cock and put on my robe and sandals, packed my passport in my overnight bag and headed out the front gate of the family compound.

The trip to the meeting took a little less than an hour. My hands shook for a good 15 minutes at first, but by the time we arrived I was alright. The meeting was to be held in an old desert fortress, in an oasis. After parking the car Carlos's father picked up my overnight bag and told me to follow him and not to speak, unless he told me to. An armed guard at the door directed us to a large hall in the back of the fortress.

As we entered the meeting room, I could see that only one man, wearing a western style suit, was present. Carlos's father talked to the man in a language that I did not understand. They haggled and at times argued. I just stood silently, in a submissive manner, with my hands behind my back and my head bowed. This is how I was told to act by Carlos's father.

Finally, the two men stopped talking and Carlos's father order me to undress. I said, "Yes Sir!" and I quickly slipped off my sandals and unbuttoned and dropped my robe. I now stood naked in a submissive manner in front of the man in the suit. He did not speak he just walked around me visually inspecting my nude body. The noises that he made seemed to indicate that he liked what he was looking at. I half smiled, so far he liked me.

The man now stepped closer and he started to physically inspect my body. He began by playing with my ass. After running his hand over my ass cheeks he gave my ass several hard slaps. A mild pain ran though my body and I physically tensed up. He than inspected my back and my arms, squeezing each muscle that he touched, before he looked over my head and inspected my teeth with his fingers.

Next, he man handled the muscles of my chest and waist and finally ending his inspection of my nude body by playing with my now hard and throbbing cock and squeezing my balls really hard. The pain made me grit my teeth.

The man raised my chin and looked into my eyes, just before he squeezed my balls really hard one more time. The pain almost lifted me off the ground. He than released his grip and my body relaxed. The man looked pleased with my naked body and my physical reactions to his brutal inspection.

The man walked over to Carlos's father and shook his hand. It seems that the man approved of me and he was ready to deal. The two men talked for a few more minutes and than shook hands again. They had come to some sort of an agreement.

I was now told to relax by Carlos's father and to come forward and to get on my knees at the front of the meeting table. Being on my knees made me just tall enough to put my arms on the top of the table and I was handed a several page contract in English. It was a slave contract. I only got a chance to read part of the first page. It started that I was willingly selling my self into slavery for a period of 5 years. It wasn't really true, but I was in no position to argue. I was told to sign the contract on three different pages. I did as I was told.

At this point, I knew that I now belonged to the man in the suit, he was my master. It was my job to please him. At least that is what I thought my new duties would be.

I was told to stand up and I assume a submissive stance in front of the table. As I stood naked and silent, I heard several people enter the room. I was ordered by the man in the suit to turn around and I obeyed. I now was almost face to face with Carlos, who was being held by two armed guards, one on each side of him. I wanted to hug him, but I knew that I couldn't. I now did not belong to Carlos any more.

Carlos looked like he had been beaten up. One of his eyes was black and he seemed to have several bruises on his face and neck. He smiled at me and said, "Thank you James for saving my life, I will wait for you." With that brief comment the guards took him away.

Carlos's father walked up to me and shook my hand. "Thank you for helping my son. You now belong to the Hussiens. After you are trained and sold they will release my son. He than kissed my hand and started to walk out of the room. I was now left standing naked, in front of the man who had just bought me, worrying what was to become of me, now that I was a slave.

As Carlos's father left the room, the mood of the man in the suit changed, he stopped smiling and he ordered a guard to tie my arms behind my back. He than had two of his guards, one on each side, take me into another part of the fortress. The guards escorted me into a large dimly lit room, half full of large pillows. The two guards threw me face down, on a pile of pillows on one side of the room and I was told not to move. I laid motionless and silent, face down on the pillows for about 20 minutes, when someone entered the room. Out of the corner of my eye I could see that he was a very muscular, bare chested guard and he was carrying some type of short whip that had many strands.

Suddenly, I felt the sting of the whip on my bare ass. I repeatedly squirmed in pain, as more blows hit my ass and my back. After about 15 minutes, of mostly light whipping, followed by several hard blows, the guard stopped and with out a word he left the room. The pain of the whipping continued to sting my body.

As the fear of not knowing what was going to happen to me next started to make my arms shake, I heard about half a dozen men enter the room. They all stood behind me and I could not see who they were. They talked in a foreign language and occasionally laughed a little. Some of the men started to caress my naked body and at times slap my bare ass really hard. The whipping that I had received had made my skin very sensitive and I yelled each time that they slapped my ass. My reactions only seemed to encourage the men to laugh and to slap my ass harder and harder.

After only a few minutes the men stopped slapping my ass and seemed to leave me alone while they talked in a group behind me. I sensed that the men were not done with playing with me and I did not have to wait long before I felt two hands part my ass cheeks, while several greased fingers were shoved deep into my asshole. Right after the greased fingers were withdrawn I felt a hard cock start to probe my asshole. Suddenly, the man entered me in one deep stroke and he continued to violently fucked me, until he was spent. The other men followed his example and fucked me long and hard for at least the next 2 hours. I squirmed, moaned and sometimes yelled. Any time that I showed any sign that the men were hurting me it only encouraged them to hurt me even more.

I didn't like to think about it, but having so many hard cocks up my ass was making me hornier than hell and most of the time that these men were fucking me I spent on mentally stopping myself from cumming. I came close to losing my load twice before the men stopped. I didn't know who these men were, but I had enough experience in life to know that they wanted to hurt and degrade me, not turn me on and get me off. So, I played the role of a victim the best that I could.

After all the men had fucked me one or more times they stopped and lifted me off of the pile of pillows and forced me to knell on the tile floor next to a drain. Most of the men who had fucked me left the room and a new group of men, who looked like soldiers, entered the room. The new men made a circle around me and one of them unzipped his pants and steps forward. The man said in broken English, "Open your mouth Boy!" "Yes Sir!" The man put his limp cock in my mouth and he said, "Drink boy." I gagged as I felt the taste of urine. I swallowed as fast as I could until the man was done with me and he withdrew his cock. Another man stepped forward and as he started to piss down my throat I could feel the warm flow of urine hitting my back, my chest and my ass, as the other soldiers pissed on me After they were through they laughed at me as I knelt naked on the tile floor with beads of piss running down my body.

It seemed that the soldiers were now done with me, at least for now and they started to file out of the room. The last soldier to leave walked up to me and slapped me across the face really hard and than he told me to not move.

I knelt on the floor, naked with piss dripping off me, for another half hour or so, before someone came into the room. It was a very old lady. She told me in English to follow her. She led me outside the fortress to what looked like a crude outdoor shower. A guard suddenly appeared and he untied my arms and told me to stand still. The old lady appeared with a bucket of soapy water and a big sponge. She quickly went to work washing down my whole body. As she washed every inch of my naked body, she would at times caress my ass and play with my balls and cock. The guard thought that seeing the old lady play with me was very funny and he laughed.

After I was allowed to take a brief shower, the old lady handed me a towel and I dried off. The guard now dismissed the old lady and than led me to a cell like room in the back of the fortress. The room was small and it only had one small window. The window had bars on it. The room had a toilet and only two pieces of furniture, one small cot and a dresser. The guard put shackles on my ankles that bound my feet close together, so I could not walk. He than ordered me to get some sleep and that the colonel would come to get me early the next day. As I tried to get some sleep, I recalled what had happened to me. I had only been a slave for a few hours and I had already been whipped, gang raped, used as a human urinal, pissed on and fondled by an old lady. My hands started to shake as I wondered, would every day of my slavery be like this one?

Chapter 7:

TRAINING

Early the next morning, just after sunrise, I was awaken by the feel of someone ripping the covers off of me. Startled, I looked up to see a man in a military uniform bending over me. "Sit up Boy!" "Yes Sir." The man now unlocked the shackles on my ankles. "Stand up Boy!" I quickly got to my feet, bowed my head and put my hands behind my back. "Boy step forward two steps." "Yes Sir!" I did as I was told and stood submissively waiting for my next order. The early morning sunlight was shinning though the small window in the room directly on my naked body.

The man just silently stared at me for several minutes, before speaking. "Boy, I'm glad to see that you at least have a basic knowledge of how to act in the presence of your superiors. We are getting off to a good start.

My name is Colonel Caffa and I am a retired officer of the French Foreign Legion. I have been hired to train you for the next 6 months, to be a total slave. I will train you to be a slave that any real master would be proud to own.

"During your training I will be your master, your training master. I own you and you will do anything that I say. Pleasing me will become the focus of your life. You will exist only to serve and please me, your master. Nothing else will matter to you. Do you understand what I am saying Boy!" "Yes Sir!"

"While I am training you, you will address me as Sir! You will only speak when I ask you a question. When you have permission to speak, you will end each sentence with Sir! Do you understand me Boy!" "Yes Sir!" "Now Boy prepared to be inspected, put your hands at your side and stare straight ahead." "Yes Sir!"

"Now Boy I don't know much about you at present, but I am going to find out a few things right now." To start my inspection my new master silently walked around me several times visually inspecting my naked body. After he seemed satisfied, he started to physically inspect me starting with my teeth and proceeding down my naked body, probing, grabbing, slapping and tickling ever square inch of me, until he had inspected my feet. I was now told to spread my legs and bend over. "Yes Sir!" As I bent over my master started to lightly massage the crack of my ass, which caused my body to squirm and shake. I than felt several wet fingers slid into my ass and start to probe and massage my prostate gland. My cock got throbbing hard and I started to moan. As my master withdrew his fingers, my body relaxed and I was ordered to stand up.

My master seemed to be done with his physical inspection of my body, but I was soon to learn that he was not done with me. "Boy, raise your arms above your head." "Yes Sir!"

My master walked out of the room. In a few minutes he came back with a whip in his hands. It looked like the same whip that had been used on me the night before. My master walked around to stand in back of me and I closed my eyes and waited to feel the sting of the whip. The first strike of the whip landed on my bare ass and my body tensed up. As blows fell on my back, ass and than the back of my legs, I gritted my teeth and my body began to squirm.

Suddenly, after about 10 minutes of whipping my master stopped and he just stood behind me and didn't say a thing. After a few minutes of silently standing, with my hands behind my head, my master walked around to stand in front of me. The first blow hit my chest and than my waist and finally the front of my legs. For the next 10 to 15 minutes my master lightly whipped both the front and back of my naked body. When my master was done he put the whip on the dresser and he told me to put my arms down and to stand submissively again. As my master walked around me physically inspecting the damage of his whipping, my whole body could still feel the sting of the whip. A mild pain pulsated though out my body.

"Well Boy, I am finding out a lot about you today. You have a great body, good bodily reactions and you can handle a good deal of pain. Most masters would find you to be very entertaining and that is good. A slave only exists to please his master."

"Now Boy, get on your knees in the proper position for a slave. "Yes Sir!" I dropped to my knees, put my hands behind my back and bowed my head. "Now Boy, I will explain what I intend to do with you these next 6 months. I will start by breaking you just like a cowboy would break a wild horse and than I will remold you, in mind and body to be a total slave. You will forget all that stuff about having rights and being treated fairly. You will learn that you are a slave and that you exist only to serve and please your master. Your life will have no other meaning. Now Boy, repeat after me, I am a slave," "I am a slave." "I exist only to please and serve my master." "I exist only to please and serve my master." "Repeat what you have just said, over and over, until I tell you to stop." "Yes Sir!" "I am a slave. I exist only to serve and please my master. I am a sl---"

My master had me repeat the words, over and over again, for the next 15 minutes. When I was ordered to stop, my master said, "Boy you are only saying the words today, but at the end of your training you will believe every word that you say. When I am though training you, you will know that you are a slave and your whole life will be focused on serving and pleasing your master." "Do you understand

Boy!" "Yes Sir, I understand Sir!" This routine became part of my training program. Every day I was required to knell naked on the floor and repeat, over and over again for a 15 minutes a day that, "I am a slave. I exist only to serve and please my master."

My new master seemed satisfied with me, so far. He left the room again for several minutes. When he returned he locked a metal collar around my neck. "Boy, this is your slave collar. It is an electronic, high tech device that let me know where you are at all times. It is water proof, shock proof, knife proof and tamper proof. It is indestructible.

So if you ever have any stupid ideas about escaping, forget them. You are a slave for the next 5 years. Do you understand what I have just said Slave!" "Yes Sir!

After only a few hours in the fortress with my new master he had me put on a light cotton robe and some sandals. I was only told that we were going for a ride. My master took me to his home, near a small military base, in an isolated area. My master's house was to be my home for the next 6 months. The house was a stone and wood two story structure that looked like it had been well cared for. That night I slept at the foot of my master's bed. My first duty in the morning was sucking off my new master, which was a job that I really liked. My new master was a man who was in his late 40's, but he was in great physical shape. He was about 6'2" in height and I would say he weighed a little over 200 pounds. He was a ruggedly good-looking man. I learned to really enjoy the times that he rewarded me by letting me please his cock. It got so that I dreamed about those moments.

My first few days of training were spent in learning my household duties and in telling my master all about my past life. I knelt submissively at my master's feet for hours telling him every detail of my past life. He showed a great deal of interest in the years that I spent living with my two daddies. He said that being a daddy's boy was good for me it made me easier to train as a slave. In my master's opinion, being a good daddy's boy had half way trained my mind to be a good man slave. It was during these first few days of training that I started to see that my master was a strict, but fair man.

After only a short week my master had trained me in how to manage his house and he know all he wanted to know about me. Now my physically and mental training would begin. My master got up at sunrise and he expected me to be awake and knelling naked at the foot of his bed. After we showered and I cared for any sexual needs my master may have I prepared the first meal of the day.

When my master had finished his meal I was allowed 20 minutes to eat and than I was to wash the dishes and put everything away. After eating his meal my master liked to read for about an hour in the living room. When I was done with cleaning up after the first meal of the day I was expected to go into the living and knell by my master's chair and wait for him to have something for me to do.

After my master was though reading he would order me to put on my running clothes and we would join the Moroccan Army soldiers, from the near by army base, for a several mile run though the local foothills. My master did not think much of the Moroccan Army. "Boy the Moroccan Army is nothing but shit. They are not a real fighting force. They are only good for parades. I would never depend on them to help me in a military situation. But, they are good for some things like running."

After running it was time for mental training. At times my master would have me do stupid things like pick up a large rock and talk it down up a hill and than bring it back down again, over and over. This was to train me to not think about what I was told to do, but just to focus on doing the task as well as I could.

Yoga was part of my mental training. My master said, "Boy you have to know how to control your body and mind. Sometimes your master will have no use for you and you will be required to stand or knell for long periods of time and you have to know how to mentally and physically handle such an inactive state." I was also told that a slave that can handle such a situation will earn his master's respect.

The second week of my training my master added massage to my program. Once a week a professional masseur would give me lessons in massage. Mr. Leon was a friend of my master and he had been hired to teach me the art of massage. My master believed that a good man slave needed to know how to give his master a full body massage.

Mr. Leon was an expert masseur and I learned a lot from him. He was also good for other things. Mr. Leon was paid in two ways for his services. He was paid for his lessons and he was allowed to use me for his pleasure after the lessons. I soon found out that my teacher was a hard core top man and he made good use of my pretty slave ass. It seems that he liked my ass so much that he convinced my master that I could use two lessons per week. I became a better masseur each week and my pretty ass got a good workout too.

In mid morning, I was required to fix and serve the second meal of the day. After I had cleaned up after the meal I returned to kneeling naked by my master's chair. An hour after the noon day meal my master took me to work out in his own home gym. The gym was in a large room in the basement of my master's home. It was very well outfitted and my master really put me though my paces. His goal was to change my boyish body to a muscular mans body. He told me he was going to add 30 pounds of defined muscle to my frame in the next 6 months. I really liked the idea of building up my body. My two daddies did not go to the gym and they did not want me to build up my body. Carlos liked my natural body and Brad knew that my smooth, hung, boyish body was part of my image. My image was a money maker for him. So, neither of them liked the idea of me going to the gym. But, now I had a master who said that it was O.K. and I really put myself into it and I wanted to please him by reaching his goal.

My master was a strict task master those first few months. I wasn't able to always do as he said and he would whip me. Whipping became part of my training program.

The whipping sessions I found out were not just for punishment, they were to conditions my body to deal with pain. Each whipping was more intense and painful than the one before. The sessions not only caused me to squirm, yell and some times cry, but they also scared me mentally. You see, as my body adjusted to the pain I began to get sexually turned on. As the whipping sessions continued my cock got harder and harder. My sexual reactions to being whipped were something, that at first, I had trouble mentally dealing with. Was I becoming a stone cold masochist?

My master would at times show that he recognized that I had made good progress and he would compliment me or reward me by letting me cum. Sometimes my master would not let me cum for a full month. He was of the opinion that a horny slave will serve his master best. He was right of course, he was always right. I did put more effort into my duties and training when I was horny.

Even the pleasure of cumming was turned into a training period. Each time I was allowed to cum my master tried to train me mentally to cum without touching myself. I was told that if I succeeded in getting off by using my mind I would be rewarded. The first time that I was able to do it my master gave me the reward that I wanted he fucked me for two hours straight. My master may be middle aged, but his big cock works as good as any young man.

My training program did not remain the same. When I would reach a goal that my master set for me, another stage in my training would open up. After several months of training one interesting change was made in my training program, it concerned sex. The change involved the used of the Moroccan soldiers.

My master had no use for the Moroccan soldiers as a fighting force, but he did have a use for them in my training program. My master was very close to the officer who commanded the soldiers in the camp next to his home. He had served in Morocco as an officer in the Legion and he had many connections in the Moroccan Army. He used his influence to get the use of some of the Moroccan soldiers to help train me.

The Moroccan soldiers knew that I was the colonel's slave and from the looks in their eyes at different times, I could tell that they wanted to use me for their pleasure. It was a task that I would be eager to perform, so when my master told me that he was going to let the soldiers use me, I though that I was going to be used to please the soldiers was really starting to turn me on.

Early one morning, during the fourth month of my training, my master told me not to fix the first meal of the day. He said that he had a challenge for me today. I was told to put on a part of sandals and nothing else. I quickly did as I was told. My master than handcuffed my hands behind my back and than told me to follow him. I followed my master out of the front door and down the hill to the soldier's camp. I could see that about 30 soldiers were in formation on the parade field and my master headed straight for them. I felt a little nervous at first. I was going to be put on display totally naked in front of a formation of soldiers. I did not know what to expect. I only knew that my master always knew what he was doing and that I would be alright.

When we walked up to the formation all of the soldiers were staring at me. My master told me to face the soldiers and to bow my head. I did as I was told. When my master bought me out to this field I was very nervous, but not the idea of 30 soldiers staring at my naked body had an affect. A surge of sexual energy started to run though my body and my big cock got half hard. I mentally tried to relax and my cock started to relax.

My master walked, up and down, in front of the soldiers talking in French. Every once in a while he would point at me and some of the soldiers would laugh a little. What was happening I did not know, I did not speak French.

After my master had talked to the soldiers they went on their morning run, the same early morning run that I and my master usually were part of. My master told me to follow him into one of the barracks. I followed my master a small room in the back of the building and I was uncuffed. He ordered me to sit on the floor with my back against the wall and remain silent. I sat down and started to use my mental training to relax my body and mind. As I sat on the floor my master walked outside and talked to someone in French.

After about an hour my master came back into the room and he put a bath towel on the floor. I was ordered to kneel on the towel and my master told me what I was to do. "Boy you are going to be of some use to the Moroccan Army today. You are going to suck off any of the soldiers in this barrack that want their cocks sucked. Do you understand Boy!" "Yes Sir!" "And Boy you better do a good job."

I didn't have long to wait before the soldiers returned from their run and started to change out of their sweaty jogging clothes. Each naked soldier walked right pass me on their way to the shower room. A line of soldiers quickly formed in front of me. The first soldier was a young man of about 20 years old and he smiled at me as he put his stiff cock in my face. This was probably going to be his first blow job and I was eager to make him feel good. I swallowed his cock down to the hair in one stroke. The young soldiers moaned and his body shook so much that I though he was going to lose his balance. He only lasted about a minute before he shot his load down my throat.

The second soldier was just a teenager. He probably was 18 years old of so, he had red hair and a very pretty 9 inch cock that was already hard and throbbing. He held me by the back of my head as I sucked his cock. He was like the first soldier. He was so horny that he got off really fast. The taste of warn, sweet cum flowing down my throat had my big cock throbbing like crazy.

Most of the soldiers were so horny that it was easy to get them off and none of them gave me any trouble. I was soon horny that I could have sucked them off all day, but after about 20 of them had gotten their rocks off my master called a halt this suck session and I was told to follow my master home. As I walked naked though the barracks many of the soldiers that I had sucked off slapped me on my bare ass. I just smiled and followed my master out the door.

After that day, running with the soldiers was never the same. The soldiers would smile at me and they looked at my ass when ever I and my master ran with them. They had used the colonel's slave and they wanted more. I hoped that my master would reward me again like that, but it is his decision.

I didn't have to wait long for a new challenge that involved the Moroccan soldiers. Several weeks later my master arranged for me to massage some of the soldiers on a regular basis. He wanted me to get some massage experience.

A massage table was set up in the little room near the showers in the barrack. A bare mattress was also put on the floor of the room. Each massage session was for one hour. I was to massage each soldier for half an hour and than for the next half hour the soldier was allowed to use me for his pleasure if he wanted too. I was eager to tackle this new challenge. The way the soldiers had been looking at and slapping my ass I knew that I was going to get royally fucked.

The first day of my new duty I went though my regular routine of fixing meals, running with the soldiers, weight training and household duties. In the early afternoon I was to begin my massage duties. I followed my master's instructions for the sessions. I stripped naked and put on only a pair of sandals. Wearing only my slave collar and the sandals I walked out the door of my master's house, down the hill and across the parade field to the barrack. On my way to the barrack several soldiers looked at my naked body and they started to grab and play with their crotches. They knew that they were finally going to get a chance to fuck me and they looked really eager.

My first client was a stocky sergeant. He walked into the room wearing only a towel. He had just taken a shower. He walked and acted like a man who was use to being in charge. The sergeant took off his towel, exposing a half hard 8 inch cock and he laid face down on the massage table without saying a word. I took this as a sign that he did not speak English.

I gave the soldier a deep tissue massage. The soldier was a perfect subject. No matter how hard I massaged him he did not complain. When the half hour massage was over the sergeant got off the table and looked at my naked body and half smiled. He walked up to me and grabbled by the hair on the back of my head and led me over to the mattress on the floor. I was pushed face down onto the mattress and I remained silent and still. The sergeant then started to caress my naked body, until he started to focus on my ass. He than got up and walked over to my massage table and grabbed a jar of lube. He applied a large gob of lube on his already hard cock. He stroked his cock several times as he looked at my pretty ass.

The soldier rode my ass for the next half hour before he shot his load. After he was finished with me he withdrew and slapped my ass several times and than he got up and walked out of the room. The whole time he was with me he had not said a thing or shown any form of emotions. He was a real cold fish, but he could really fuck and that is what really mattered to me.

My next client was the 18 year old, red headed soldier with a pretty 9 inch cock. I had sucked him off a few days ago. He walked into the room smiling and he shook my hand. He did not seem to speak much English so I indicated to him that he was to get on the table face down. Massaging him was a pleasure. He was a good looking young man and he had beautiful smooth skin, a pretty natural body and a great looking ass. The young soldier seemed to like being massaged and he would get playful. At times, when I was massaging him, he would reach out and fondle me, or caress my bare ass. I never tried to stop him I was here to please the soldiers in any way that they wanted me to.

After the message the young soldier got off the table and walked right up to me. He grabbed the back of my head and than he kissed me for several minutes, while he fondled me. I couldn't help it but this young man was really turning me on. My big cock was throbbing up and down.

Suddenly, the young man did the unexpected, he walked over to the mattress on the floor and he laid face down. He looked up at me and spoke the only English words that I had heard him speak so far. "Fuck me Sir, fuck me."

I quickly greased my cock, spread his cheeks and started to enter him. He let out a slight moan as my cock slid deep into his ass. I started to take slow deep strokes and the young man started to moan and shake. This young soldier was not a virgin he had been fucked in the past and he liked being a bottom.

I fucked the young soldier for the next half hour, but I did not cum. I did not have my master's permission to cum. After I had withdrawn and gotten to my feet I bent over and helped the young soldier to get up. After he was on his feet I looked down at the mattress and noticed that the soldier had shot his load on the mattress. This boy was a born bottom and he really liked being fucked.

The boy was different from the other soldiers and I was to quickly find out how different. As the boy got to his feet he put his arms around me and gave me a long, deep kiss just before he said in broken English, "You are Colonel's slave and I like that. I would like to be Colonel's slave." With that he kissed me one more time and than he smiled and left the room.

The third and last client of the day was boring compared to the first two. I ended up sucking him off after the massage and he left the room. The fresh memory of the young red haired soldier made me smile as I cleaned up the room. He was different from the other soldiers, but in a way he was a lot like me.

As usual, when I got back to my master's house I told him everything that had happen. My master seemed especially interested with what I said about the young red haired soldier.

During my last month of training I learned that my master was not done in finding interesting ways to use the soldiers to train me. Early one morning my master said, "Boy, you are going on a special diet today. The diet is designed to trim and define your body and get you ready to be sold. For the next two weeks the only things that you are going to have to eat is piss and cum."

"Every day, for the next two weeks, I will take you naked over to the barrack. You will knell on a bath towel on the floor of the bathroom and twice a day you will suck off the soldiers and also let them piss down your throat. Cum and piss are the only things that you are going to have to eat in the next two weeks. Cum is full of protein and piss is full of vitamins and minerals that the body did not need. Boy you are going to learn the value of cock. For the next two weeks cock is going to feed you and keep you alive. Do you understand Boy!" "Yes Sir!"

So, for the next two weeks I lived off of soldiers cock. The first few days were a little rough, but I adjusted to the change and I started to look forward to going to the barrack. Each day I sucked off at least 20 soldiers and had about 10 or 12 soldiers piss down my throat. By the time the two weeks were up I had lose 14 pounds and my body was so defined that I looked like a road map.

The last two weeks of my training I was slowly put back on my regular high protein, low carb diet. The energy that I had lost during my special diet came back and I felt great. I was a little startled the first time I looked at myself naked in a mirror. My master had reached his goal. He had added about 30 pounds of well defined muscle to my body. I looked like a completely different person. In the mirror I didn't see the hung boy that I was 6 months before, I saw a very muscular young man. I was starting to look forward to the up coming auction and I hoped that I would please my master one more time by bring a high price.

My master had told me the truth that first day at the fortress. He said that he was going to train me to be a total slave and he has succeeded. I no longer feel or think like an average person. I spend every waking minute of my day thinking only of serving and pleasing my master. Nothing else matters to me.

I think my master was right when he told me, "Boy after training you for only 6 months I can already see that you are a natural born submissive. You are a closet slave and I just dragged you out of your closet and made you what you were meant to be, a man's property."

My existence as my master's slave has made me feel very content and safe. I have trouble relating to the work a day world of the average person. I don't have the same worries and concerns of every day people. I serve my master and he protects and cares for me. I have no worldly problems such as having a career in the business world, paying taxes, caring about what is happening in the world and the local community, or about what other people think. I only care about what my master wants me to do. I feel very content with my new station in life and I see no reason why I would want to change it. I am a slave, the property of my master and that is my life.

Chapter 8:

THE AUCTION

The trip by car to the site of the auction took 3 hours. The auction was to be held at a former French air base in an isolated area of Morocco. Driving up to the main building for the event we could see at least a dozen private jets on the airfield runway. The event parking lot was beginning to fill up.

We had arrived two hours before the pre-show and my master decided that I should rest before the show. My master found me a bed in a small room in one of the buildings at the auction site. He wanted me to get a little sleep before I was to be put on display. My master wanted me to look refreshed when I stood naked on the display platform during the pre-show. He told me to try to get some sleep and he would be back for me in about an hour and a half. I took off my cotton robe and sandals and crawled naked into bed.

I managed to relax but it was hard for me to get to sleep. My body was tense. The reality of the day was beginning to cause my sexual energy level to rise. The thought that in just a few hours I was to be standing naked on an auction block, in front of several hundred men, ready to be sold to the highest bidder had caused my cock to get throbbing hard and I found it hard to get any sleep.

I was relieved to hear the footsteps of my master returning. I hadn't been able to sleep I was only able to close my eyes and rest. My body was tense and my cock was still hard. My master ordered me to get up and to follow him. I quickly obeyed and I was soon following my master naked down a long hallway to what turned out to be a large, two story room. I was led to a small round platform that stood about one foot off of the floor. The small platform was surrounded by a temporary rope barrier that stood about three feet tall. My master told me to mount the platform. After I got on the small platform I was ordered to stand with my feet about two feet apart. My master than shackled my ankles to the platform.

My master now put my auction number chain around my neck. I was to be number 17. He than gave me my orders, "Boy this is the pre-show. You will stand on this platform, with your hands at your side and look directly forward. During the next two hours potential buyers will review the slaves to be sold tonight. If a possible buyer is interested in a closer review of your body the attendant that is assigned to you will let him do a physical inspection. This pre-show is designed to give potential buyers a better idea of which slaves they will want to bid on at the auction tonight. Do you understand Boy!" "Yes Sir!"

My master turned me over to the attendant who was assigned to look after me and than he left. My master was to be the auctioneer tonight and he had to get his staff ready for the show. I felt a certain amount of pride in the fact that my own master was the one who was going to sell me tonight.

I stood naked on my platform with a throbbing hard on, as the other slaves were shackled to their platforms. Over all, about 20 slaves were put on display. Since I was on the outer edge of the room I was able to see all of the slaves that were to be sold. The slaves on display were a mixed group of ages and races. They ranged from very boyish pretty boys to very rugged looking, semi hairy men. The one that looked the oldest, an Asian slave, was about in his late 20's and the youngest, a blond smooth bodied, pretty boy could not have been older than about 18. I was happy to see that none of them could match my muscular and well-define body or my big dick. I smiled, I wanted very badly to score the highest price tonight and make my master proud of me.

After waiting only about 15 minutes the potential buyers came into the hall. The men were all dressed casually and they walked among the slaves to be sold, looking over each one and sometimes writing notes down on each slave. I was surprised to see that some of the potential buyers had brought along their personal slaves. The slaves were naked just like me, but with a small difference, they had red slave collars, not black like the slaves to be sold tonight. A crowd soon formed around me and my attendant started to get requests to physically inspect my naked body. The first person to inspect me was young looking man that looked like he was in his early 30's. He had a very stern look in his eyes and he was all business. He inspected me just like a rancher would inspect a prized stallion that he was interested in buying. He smiled a bit after he was though as he wrote down a few notes on his pre-show form.

Having one after the other of the buyer's man handle my naked body was something that really turned me on. It kept my cock throbbing hard during the hours of the pre-show. My master had trained me in what to expect at this auction. Only one unexpected event happened that caught me by surprise. It did not startle me it just made me smile a little. It concerned a slave that one of the buyers had bought to the show. He was a good-looking, dark haired, nicely hung slave in his mid-twenties. It seems that I had quiet an effect on his cock. He stood in front of me, on the other side of the rope barrier, just staring directly at me while he licked his lips and his hard cock just throbbed wildly up and down like he was a dog in heat. I wondered if his master would take note that his slave thought that I was really hot.

Before the pre-show was over I had been physically inspected by almost 30 men. My naked and aroused body had been caressed, fondled, tickled, slapped, grabbed and probed. Over 30 men had inspected my asshole with their greased fingers and in some cases their whole hand. Two of the men actually recognized me as a well known porn star. It was a fact that seemed to impress them. As the crowd left the hall I could not help but smile. I had been the main attraction of the pre-show and that should guarantee that I will bring a high price at the auction tonight.

After the pre-show was over and the hall had been cleared of the potential buyers my master unshackled me from the platform. As I stepped down to the floor my master grabbed my balls and lightly squeezed them. My body tensed up. "Boy you did very well. The buyers paid a lot of attention to you." He smiled and released my balls. "It is going to be really interesting to see what price you bring at the auction tonight."

It would be another five hours before the auction was to begin and my master wanted me primed and ready. After taking a shower my master and I had some dinner before my master was to take me over to the auction hall for a little rehearsal.

During dinner my master decided that it was the right time to tell me what it was all about. That is the system that I was now part of. "Boy, this system was developed about 8 years ago to fill a need. To fill a need is the reason most new business concepts come into existence. The need was to supply well-trained man slaves to rich, over worked, gay business executives, who were into the leather scene."

"These men do not have much free time on their hands. They do not have the time or the skills to find a good man slave to service their needs. The system finds and professionally trains high quality man slaves and sells them for a period of 5 years."

"Why does the system work so well? It is because all sides win in this arrangement. The master selling the slave gets upwards of 50% of the selling price. In your case the Hussiens get 50%. The slave gets the remaining 50% of the selling price. The master gets his money in 5 yearly installments and the slave gets one half of his money when he completes his contract in a Swiss bank account. The other half of the slave's money is put into a trust under his control. But slave cannot take out any money from his trust until he is 40 years old. It is a retirement trust that is designed to provide for the slave in later years."

"The master who buys the slave gets a good-looking, well trained man slave, for a price of, let's say, $60,000 to $100,000 a year. For most of our clients the cost of a fine man slave is no more than pocket change to them. It is no more than the cost of hiring a good butler for a year and a butler won't provide the level of personal service that a well-trained slave will.

"The slave that our clients buy will take care of their house and their cocks better than any lover or sugar boy would. The master never has to buy the slave a new car or take him to Europe and best of all he never has to argue with them about anything. A slave is the best servant a rich gay man could have.

"The masters here tonight have had a good year financially and I believe that I can sell you for at least a half a million dollars. You are top quality and the clients that we deal with really like quality."

As I sat naked with a throbbing hard on just across the table from my master I found it hard to believe that anyone was going to pay half a million dollars to have me suck their cock for the next five years. I was just a good looking mass of raging hormones, who was use to thinking more with his big cock than his head. Why anyone would pay a small fortune to use me as their sex slave was still hard for me to understand.

Even if it seemed to be way out in left field for me the idea that I would come out of this arrangement with a good deal of money made me feel a lot better. I managed a small smile.

The auction hall was an old airplane hanger not to far from the room that was used for the pre-show. My master had me put on a pair of sandals so that I could walk on the hot ass fault of the airfield runway. I walked behind my master with beads of sweat running down my naked body. Several of the potential buyers saw us and they stopped what they were doing and just stared at my naked body.

The airplane hanger had been made ready for the auction. It had a large stage, with curtains and a long runway that extended halfway into the audience section. The room must have contained at least 200 seats, arranged in rows of ten.

My master led me backstage and he showed me the little room where I would wait for my turn on the stage. The room was small, with only enough room for a cot like bed and a lamp. The room door was marked with my auction number, number 17.

My master now led me though the routine that I was to follow. My number would be coming up and the hall attendant would knock on the door of my room and tell me that I had 3 minutes. During these 3 minutes I was to put on my number chain, compose myself and walk out to stand behind the curtain and wait for my number to be called. When I hear my number I was to walk out on the runway and mount the auction platform at the end of the runway. At this point my master would introduce me and point out my best points as the auction platform slowly rotated. After my introduction and review my master wanted my cock to perform. When I was asked to I was to mentally cause my cock to shot a big load. After I had shot my load the bidding would begin.

After I was sold I was to walk down a section of stairs to the right of the auction platform and an attendant would take me to a holding room. My new master would claim me as his new property after the auction was over and payment had been made.

The next half hour my master walked though what I was to do tonight, I sat in my small room and waited for my number to be called and than I waited behind the curtain before I heard my number and than I walked out on the runway and mounted the platform. My master went over his introduction and pointed out my best points. The whole rehearsal felt so real that my cock wildly throbbed up and down. If my master had ordered me to cum I could have gotten off in less than half a minute.

After putting me though my paces at the auction hall my master returned me to my small room. My master gave me a glass of water with some herbal exacts in it, they were designed to make me super horny in order to guarantee that I would be able to cum without touching myself at the right moment. I drank the water and my master told me to get some sleep. My master now left to run the other slaves though the same rehearsal that I had just been though. It seems that my master gave me special consideration when he ran me though what I had to do. I smiled and drifted off to sleep.

When the time of the auction was approaching my master woke me up and had me put on only a part of sandals, before I followed my master over to the auction hall. The slaves and the potential buyers were already filing into the airfield hanger. My master led me to my waiting room and told me to sit down on the cot and get my mind in focus I had about 20 minutes before the auction began. My number was 17, but I would be the fifth slave to be on stage tonight.

I could not get any rest, the herbal drink and the fact that I had not been allowed to cum in nearly a month had me so horny that my cock was hard as a rock. I sat on my cot, with my back against the wall started to think about what was about to happen to me. I was going to be sold to a complete stranger who would be my master for the next five years. Would he be a good master or would he be a cruel master? I did not know, but instead of being scared, as I expected, I was extremely energized. I never felt so alive in my life

This was the first time in my life that I actually felt like I was worth anything. Tonight some total stranger was going to pay a small fortune for the right to own me for the next five years. When I was a high priced hustler for Brad's agency I really got off on the fact that I was paid $500 an hour to do what I like to do, please men. But, that was small change compared to the high that I now felt.

Suddenly, the attendant told me to get ready I had 3 minutes to get ready. As I got to my feet, beads of sweat started to run down my naked body, as my cock throbbed so hard that I felt like cumming right than and there. I put on my number chain and started out the door. As I walked down the hallway I could hear music being played. People in the hallway stopped what they were doing and stared at my muscular naked body and big hard cock. They seemed pleased and most of them smiled. As I stood behind the stage curtains some of the backstage crew patted me on my bare ass, tickled my balls and played with my pulsating cock. All of which made me even hornier.

As my number was called I felt a surge of sexual energy flow though my body. I parted the curtains and started to walk down the runway. All the way down the runway my big stiff cock just bounced against my stomach. I got more and more turned on as I realized that several hundred men were visually raping my naked body. The approving sounds from the audience just made me feel more energized. I smiled, as I mounted the auction platform.

As I stood on the posing platform the sounds of the audience died down, the auction was starting. The overhead lights went on and the auctioneer walked up to stand beside me. My master quickly looked over my naked body and smiled. My master looked very pleased. He than started to point out my best points and to describe how will trained I was. He finished his introduction of me by showing off one of my talents, he ordered me to cum without touching myself. I was so turned on that cumming was easy. In less than a minute I shot several streams of warm, sticky cum several feet into the air.

As cum and sweat ran down my naked body my master began the bidding. That night I sold for the highest price of the auction, $800,000 dollars. It was a figure that shocked the hell out of me, but it made my master proud of me. As the attendant led me away the audience wildly clapped. I smiled. I had pleased my master one more time and I had had the wildest experience of my life and that was all that mattered to me.

After the attendant cleaned me up he led me to a small room that was being used as a holding room for sold slaves. Three slaves that had been sold before me were sitting on wooden stools with their arms tied behind their backs. One plain mattress covered part of the floor.

The attendant tied my arms behind me and told me to sit on one of the stools and to remain silent. He told me that my new master would claim me as soon as the money transfer took place. I sat down and kept quiet. As I waited for my new master to show up I looked over the other slaves in the room. They were all calm like me except for a young pretty blond boy. He was the same blond boy that I had seen at the pre-show, the one that barely looked 18 years old. His body shook and his eyes had a scared look in them. I was to find out the reasons for his sense of fear later.

I sat silently for almost an hour before an attendant and a new master came to claim his property. An Asian man claimed a good-looking young Hispanic slave and walked out of the room.

As on sat naked on my stool I started to get a little scared. The reality of what my new master would make me do to justify the high price he had paid for me. An image of my first day of slavery, the day I was gang raped, wiped, abused and pissed on, caused my body to shake a little.

The second master to claim a slave was a completely different story. He was a good-looking, long haired blond man, who was in his 30's. He looked great, but there was something about his eyes and the vibrations that I got from him that told me he was trouble.

My eyes caught his and my body tensed up. Was this man my new master? The man smiled at me and my heart sank. I felt like I was really in trouble until the man broke eye contact with me and looked directly at the young blond pretty boy.

The blond boy moaned really loud and his body started to shake as he said, "Oh no, not you." The young slave seemed to know the man. The long haired blond master smiled a little before he walked over and claimed the scared, young man as his property. The young man's new master ordered him to stand up and he obeyed. The boy's master than untied the slave and for the next 15 minutes or so, he brutally inspected his new slave's naked body. He pulled on his nipples so hard that he yelled and he squeezed his ball until the boy started to cry.

After he was though inspecting his new property the blond master grabbed his slave by the shoulders and threw him on to the mattress. The boy's master than took off his clothes, exposing a big and hard throbbing cock. This whole brutal scene had really turned on the man. He put some lube on his hard cock and than he bent down and shoved his big cock all the way up the slave's ass. The young slave screamed and his body shook as the boy's new master shoved it to him long and hard. The more that the young slave showed that he was in pain the more his new master shoved it to him. The boy's new master really liked to inflect pain on him he really got off on it.

After the new master had fucked his slave long and hard for almost a half hour he finally shot his load up the slave's ass and he withdrew. But, he was not done. He had a crazy glazed look in his eyes. As the young slave laid motionless on the mattress his master leaned forward and put his hands on the boy's shoulders. Suddenly, the boy's master clawed his way done the boy's back, across his ass and down the back of his legs. The boy screamed and started to cry. The new master had left fingernail marks all the way down his slave's body and some of the marks were so deep that they were bleeding.

The boy was still crying as his new master yanked him to his feet. He was told to put on his robe and sandals and he obeyed. As the new master took his slave away I felt a sign of relief, thank god that brutal bastard was not my master.

The next master to enter the room was a rugged, stern looking man in his 40's. He looked straight at me and didn't say a word or smile, he just walked over to me and grabbed me by the hair on the back of my head and yanked me to my feet. When I was standing upright he let go of my hair and he looked into my eyes, "Boy I am your new master. I now own you and I expect to get a lot of use out of you. Do you understand Boy?" Yes Sir, I will serve you well Sir!" "You had better Boy, you cost me a lot and I intend to get my money worth out of you."

My new master now started to inspect me, he at first just walked around me and than he ran his hands all over my naked body. My big cock remained throbbing hard. This fact was not lost on my new master. He grabbed my hard cock and said, "Good, you are a really horny slave. Boy how many times can you got off in one day?" "I can cum up to 10 times in one day, if you want me to Sir!" "Boy how long can you go without cumming?" "I can go without cumming for months, if that is what you want Sir!" "Boy how experienced are you at cock sucking and are you a good fuck?" "I am a very experienced cock sucker and I have been told that I am a really great fuck Sir!"

My new master smiled, he seemed to like my answers. He started to unzip his pants and he pulled out a nice 8 inch cock. "O.K. experienced cock sucker let's see how good you are. Get on you knees Boy!" "Yes Sir." I had swallowed my master's cock clear down to his hair and began to give him the best blow job that I had ever given anyone. I started to think of what a lucky slave I was to have been sold to a master with such a nice man sized cock.

After sucking on my new master's beautiful man cock for about 10 minutes, I felt his legs shake and he started to moan. My master let out a load moan and his cock started to swell just before started to shot a big load of man cum down my throat. I licked the last drops of cum off of his still hard cock before I was stopped. My master grabbed me by the hair on the back of my head and he pulled me onto my feet. I bowed my head and put my hands behind my back.

"Boy you were not kidding when you said you were a good cock sucker. Now I am going to find out what sort of fuck you are. My master led me over to the mattress and ordered me to lay face down. I soon felt a greased cock slid up my ass as my body tensed up and I started to moan. After a half hour of good fucking I felt my master shot his load up my ass. I was so turned on I almost lost my load. My master withdrew and he slapped my ass several times. He seemed very pleased with my performance.

"Well Boy, you are one fantastic fuck and I intend to get a lot of good fucking out of you in the next few years. Boy, get up and put on your robe and sandals, we are going to fly to my island." Yes Sir!" As I got dressed I couldn't help but think, God, my new master has a beautiful man sized cock, he really likes to fuck me and he owns his own island. Man, I am one lucky slave.

Chapter 9:

THE ISLAND

My new master's plane was parked on the runway of the old airfield. The plane was what is called a corporate jet. Two young uniformed pilots stood near the door to the jet. As my master approached them they greeted him, "Good evening Mr. Clark was your buying trip a success?" "Yes John, as you can see it was a big success." My master grabbed me by the neck and shoved me in front of the two pilots. They both smiled. "He is sure a good looking young man, but how does he look naked?" My master smiled and said, "Well I will show you. Boy strip and let the pilots inspect you." "Yes Sir." I took off my sandals and than I unbuttoned my robe and let it drop to the ground. I now stood naked in front of the two pilots who both looked very impressed.

With out saying a word the two pilots eagerly started to physically inspect my naked body. The feel of two young, good looking men man handling my naked body caused my big cock to get rock hard. As a final act of inspection the two pilots tickled my firm balls at the same time as they watched me squirm. "He sure has a great body and a nice cock on him. You made a very good buy tonight." "Yes I know and I intend to get a lot of use out of him."

As I followed my master and the pilots into the plane my clothes were left on the ground. My master told me I would not need them from now on. I followed my master into the main cabin of the plane and he sat down in one of the over stuffed chairs. My master told me to kneel in front of him and to put my head on his lap and my arms around his waist. As the plane lifted off from the runway and started to climb I held on to my new master as he held my back in his arms.

After the plane had leveled off and the seat belt sign went off my master pulled me off of his lap and he unbuckled his seat belt. He looked at me kneeling naked at his feet for a moment, than he started to unzip his pants and pull out his big cock.

"Now Boy it's time for some more of your expert cock sucking." "Yes Sir!" I bent down and started to lick the head of my master's cock and he started to moan. As I licked up and down, both sides of his shaft his body squirmed a little. Than as I swallowed his cock clear down to his hair his body tensed up and he said, "Oh Oooh that feels sooo good. Suck it boy, suck it good.

It took me only about 5 minutes to get him off. The feel of warm, sweet cum flowing down my throat was as good as any dessert that I have ever had. After I had licked my master's cock clean, I moved back to kneel on my knees, I bowed my head and put my hands behind my back and said, "Thank you Sir!" I remained silent, waiting for my master to have further use of me.

My master seemed pleased with my performance. He ran his hand though my hair and said, "Good Boy." He than got up and walked down the aisle and into the cockpit of the plane. I knelt on the cabin floor as my master talked to the two pilots. I could only make out parts of what was said. "We can have a go at" "He is a great fuck and boy can he." "It sounds good to me."

Suddenly, the talking stopped and someone came out of the pilot's cabin and walked down the aisle. The man stopped and stood in back of me. I could hear the sounds of shoes hitting the floor and pants being unzipped. Suddenly, one of the pilots sat down completely naked in the chair right in front of me. "Look at me Boy." "Yes Sir!" I raised my head to see that the pilot was stroking his hard cock and smiling at me. "Now Boy your master has given you to me to play with and I intend to take advantage of that fact. Boy get your face down here and lick my balls." "Yes Sir!" I leaned forward and I started to slowly stroke his cock as I licked his balls. He started to squirm and moan. He liked the feel of my hot, wet tongue on his balls. After a few minutes he ordered me to suck his cock and I swallowed as much of his cock as I could shove down my throat. His whole body tensed up and he started to moan. For the next 15 minutes I tongue massaged and sucked his cock as he squirmed in his seat. Finally, the pilot could whole it no longer and he shot a big load of warm cum down my eager throat. I licked his cock clean and than I knelt submissively again on my knees and said, "Thank you Sir!"

The young pilot seemed pleased, he smiled, "Good Boy." But he was not finished with me yet. He stood up, with his cock still hard and throbbing, with a little cum still dripping down the shaft. He grabbed me by the back of my neck, pulled me to my feet and than positioned me face down in the aisle way. He than reached between my legs and grabbed me by the balls. "O.K. Boy lets lift that ass up." "Yes Sir!" As I felt him pull my balls upward I lifted my ass up only to feel a pillow slid under my hips.

The pilot released my balls and he started to caress my ass just before I felt several greased fingers enter my ass and start to massage my asshole. I relaxed and waited. Soon I felt the thrust of a greased cock as it slid deep inside of me. I squirmed and moaned as the thrust of the pilot's cock started to pick up speed. As my ass quickly adjusted to the deep thrusts of his cock I began to really enjoy being royally fucked. The pilot rode my ass in the aisle way for almost an hour before he finally came inside of me. The pilot's warm cum hit my prostrate gland and I got so turned on I almost lost my load.

After the pilot was finished with me, he got up and ran his hand down my back and he briefly played with my ass. Than he gave my bare ass a good slap and said, "Boy you are one good fuck. Don't move Boy I know someone else that will be interested in your beautiful ass." "Yes Sir!"

As the pilot entered the cockpit I could hear him talk to my master. "Well, Mr. Clark your new boy in one hell of a good fuck." "Yes I know." "Can Chuck have a go at him?" "Yes, it will be interesting to watch Chuck fuck the new boy with his big cock." "Is that alright with you Chuck?" "Hell yes Mr. Clark. I would love to fuck the shit out of your new boy."

As I heard the sound of several people leave the cabin and walk down the aisle I relax my body and waited to be fucked again. I could hear what sounded like two people sitting down in the chairs behind me and someone getting undressed. In only a short minute I felt a hand caress my ass just before I felt the head of a cock start to probe my asshole. Suddenly, a big greased cock slid deep into my ass, farther than any cock had ever gone. My body tensed up so violently that most of my body lifted off the ground. I nearly screamed as the man's big cock hit bottom. God, his cock was big.

My master and the other pilot seemed to enjoy the little show that I was putting on. I could hear sounds of approval from them, as I squirmed and moaned, as the super hung pilot fucked me long and hard. In a few minutes my ass muscles had relaxed and I started to really like being fucked by this hung pilot. The pilot didn't seem to like my sounds of pleasure and he turned me over, put my legs on his shoulders and he started to really shove it to me. I moaned and my body shook, all of which seemed to really turn on the pilot. The more that I moaned and squirmed the harder the pilot shoved it to me. Finally, after only about 10 minutes the pilot started to get close to cumming. He withdrew his cock and let it freely shoot a big load of warm, sticky cum all over my chest and stomach. The pilot looked very pleased and he bent over and kissed me. I smiled and said, "Thank you Sir!" I had pleased the pilot and that is all that mattered to me.

After being fucked by the two pilots my master seemed very pleased with me. My master and I took a quick shower together and than I slept naked with my master for several hours in a double bed that was in the back of the plane. Sleeping next to my master's warm body for the first time felt so relaxing that I quickly drifted off to sleep.

I woke up to the feel of my master's hand slapping my bare ass. He had a hungry look on his face. He ran his hand down my naked back and he started to play with my ass. I started to move my ass in a come fuck me manner and I quickly put a pillow under my hips and relaxed my body. From the moment my master's cock entered me to the moment he shot his load, I enjoyed this fucking as much as my master.

As my master got up to take a shower he told me to stay put. I just relaxed and waited for my master's next order. After my master had finished his shower he got dressed and walked out of the room and down the aisle in the direction of the cockpit. About 15 minutes later I heard someone come into the bedroom. I lifted up my head and looked to see who it was. It was both of the pilots and they were getting undressed. I smiled at them. I was going to get some more action.

As the pilots took off their underwear I could see that both of them were very eager. Both of the pilots were sporting roaring hardons. This time they had something different in mind. The hung pilot that was called Chuck slapped my bare ass and told me to get on my knees, doggy style. When I was on my knees the other pilot sat down in front of me on the bed and told me to suck his cock. As I went down on the pilot's cock I could feel the pressure of a big greased cock playing with my asshole. Suddenly, the super hung pilot entered me in one deep thrust and my body tensed up, lifting me off of the other pilot's cock. My body violently shook and I moaned as the pilot's huge cock started to move in and out of my ass.

As my body adjusted to being fucked by a foot long dick I started to suck the other pilot's cock, right down to his hair. He moaned really loud, as he ran his hands over my shoulders and back. "Good Boy, you suck cock so good."

In just about 5 minutes both pilot were getting close to cumming. I started to deep throat the pilot's cock, again and again, until he shot his wad down my throat just as the other pilot shoot his load up my ass. The sensation of having warm cum shot into both ends of me at the same time caused me to feel light headed for a moment.

The two pilots acted very pleased with me. They both ran their hands though my hair and said things like, "Boy, you're one great fuck" "Fucking right man." "I wished I was as rich as Mr. Clark. I would buy you in a minute for my personal use." These sounds of approval made me smile.

The pilots both slapped me on the ass and than they lifted me off of the bed and pointed me in the direction of the shower. After we cleaned up and showered the pilots put me to bed, before they got dressed and went back to the cockpit. I put my head down on the pillow and smiled, my master said that he had paid a lot of money for me and he was going to get his money's worth out of me and I hoped that he continued to do just that. I love being fucked and sucking dick. To an oversexed young man like me my present life is pure heaven.

It was early the next day when my master's plane touched down on an airstrip on a tropical island. I did not know where we were, it looked like it was some place in the Pacific Ocean. As the plane came to a stop on the runway my master told me to stand up. When I was standing in a submissive manner my master took a small key out of his pocket and he unlocked my slave collar and put it in his over night bag. "Boy you won't need your collar on my island." As I followed my master out of the plane, I could see that a car was parked on the runway. A man was leaning against the car. As I followed my master over to the car I could see that the man was wearing only a pair of beach sandals. He had a very muscular and trim body and he looked like he was in his late 20's. His naked body was completely hairless, except for his eyebrows and he had a silver ring on the end of his big cock.

My master introduced me to the man. His name was Karl. He was German and my master had owned him for the last 8 years. Karl was my master's number one boy. He managed my master's house and I was soon to learn he would manage me.

My master gave Karl permission to inspect me and he took advantage of the moment. Karl walked up to me and gave me a cold look just before he started to brutally inspect my naked body. Every time he squeezed or grabbed a spot on my body that caused me to squirm in pain he focused on that point until I nearly screamed. My master seemed to be a little amused at how Karl was handling me. I quickly realized that Karl did not like me much because he saw me as competition and he was just showing me that he was top boy on this island.

My master's house was a large Victorian house, with wrap around porches. Both Karl and I were ordered to bring in our master's bags. Karl took the small bags and left the heavy ones for me.

After I had bought my master's bags into the house Karl told me to stand at attention. I quickly obeyed. Karl was not done with messing with me. He walked over and started to pull on my public hair really hard, causing me to squirm and almost lift off the ground. Karl than looked at our master and said, "Sir are going to have this boy's body hair permanently shaved and his cock ringed, just like me?" "No Karl I already own a shaved and ringed slave." Karl than looked into my eyes and grabbed my balls. As he squeezed my balls really hard he asked out master, "Sir if you like I can castrate him for you." "No Karl the new boy will keep his balls." Karl now released my balls and I felt relieved.

My first encounter with Karl was anything but pleasant and in the next few months he did not lighten up a bit. Karl was my boss and he really put me though my paces. When our master did not need me I was Karl's property. With Karl as my mentor and boss I soon learned how to do every slave job on the island. When I wasn't working for our master or Karl I was to kneel naked on the living room floor and wait for new orders. Sometimes I would kneel and wait for hours before anyone had a use for me.

My first few months on the island were very much like a training camp. My master and Karl were very strict with me, very military in nature. I was given very detailed instructions and every task that I was given to do was to be done in the way that my master wanted it done. If I got something wrong I was punished. Whipping was the main punishment, but sometimes I was given a meaningless task to do over and over again, like carry several heavy books from one end of the house to the other and back again, for an hour or more. Such meaningless tasks kept me busy and amused Karl.

The physical training that my training master had started was continued. I trained with my new master and Karl. Early in the morning Karl and I would go jogging with our master on the beach. Our master wore sweats and we wore only gym socks and a pair of tennis shoes. By the time we finished our run in the hot, humid early morning air our naked bodies were covered with beads of sweat. Running naked on the beach in the early morning sunlight not only helped to keep Karl and I in shape it also gave us a good all over tan.

Weight training was something we did every other day in my master's personal gym in the basement of the main house. This was one of the only times that Karl and I wore clothes. We wore sweats just like our master. Our master told us that it was a matter of gym safety.

My master used the same weight training diet that my training master, the colonel had used. It was a high protein, low carb diet. Between the diet and our physical training all three of us were kept in top shape. Our master liked being in good shape and he took great pride in the fact that he owned two young man slaves that were in perfect physical condition.

After several months Karl started to lighten up on me. I had shown him that I was more than just a pretty face and body I was also a very hard and dependable worker. He started to treat me more as an equal and less like a homeless dog that his master had bought home. I had shown him that I knew that he was top boy and that I accepted that fact. I began to settle into my new life. I felt more relaxed and secure. I now had a home again.

The island seldom had visitors. There were only five people on the island, my master, Karl and me and two lesbians who lived on the other side of the island. The two lesbians were named Meg and Lacy. They were retired teachers who sometimes did repair work for my master.

The first time that I met Meg and Lacy it was about a month after I arrived on the island. At the time I didn't even know that they lived on the island. One day after I had finished my house duties I knelt on the floor of the living room and waited for someone to give me something to do.

As I knelt naked on the floor, with my mind focused on relaxing my body, I felt a hand on my shoulder. Someone said, "Hello, my name is Meg." I looked up to see a strange women standing in front of me. I at first didn't know what to say. I just stared at her.

Suddenly, I hear a familiar voice. "Get on your feet Boy!" It was my master. I got to my feet and assumed a submissive stance. The women in front of me stared at my naked body for a moment. "Well Mr. Clark so this is your new boy. He sure is pretty and he has a whopper of a dick on him." "If you want to Meg you can inspect him." I suddenly felt Meg run her hands over the full length of my naked body. After only a minute or so she was playing with and caressing my bare ass. "Wow, your new boy has one beautiful butt."

"Boy what is your name?" "My name is James." "Are you an American boy?" "Yes I grow up in Indiana." "Well James, I wonder, do you have a nick name?" "Yes, at one time I had a daddy master who called me sweet cheeks." "With a pretty butt like yours I can understand why someone tagged you with that nick name." "Welcome to the island sweet cheeks. I'll introduce you to my better half Lacy later. She will probably like you, especially since she thinks that all men should be well trained slaves." On hearing this comment my master laughed a little.

"Well Mr. Clark I can sure see why you bought this boy. He is one beautiful young man. Does he have any special talents that are more than just physical?" My master seemed amused at this comment. "Yes Meg he has one talent that you met find interesting. "Boy how long has it been since you last came?" "It has been almost a month Sir!" My master looked at my hard throbbing cock and smiled. "Well Boy shot your load." "Yes Sir!" I closed my eyes and mentally thought about cumming and in less than a minute my body tensed up and I started to grit my teeth as my cock erupted and shoot several streams of warm, sticky cum several feet into the air. As cum splashed down on my body and the floor, Meg started to wildly clap. "Wow this boy is really full of cum." I smiled and said, "Thank you Sir!"

In the next few months I met Lacy and slowly Meg and Lacy became my friends. Both Meg and lacy seemed to like my nick name. When ever the two women were at my master's house they liked to call me sweet cheeks and pat me on my bare ass. It amused my master and Karl so it was alright with me. Being of service to my master was my life.

Chapter 10:

KARL

My master was a very successful international businessman. He had business interests all over the world. My master ran his business empire from a computer room in one of the upstairs bedrooms. He would sit at a desk in the room and constantly phone and e-mail people all around the world.

Every few months my master had to leave on a business trip and he ordered the corporate jet to pick him up on the island. Both I and Karl enjoyed the times that the corporate plane would set down on the island runway. We both knew that the two pilots would want some action before they left. When the pilots were on the island our master always give me and Karl the job of entertaining them in the guest house down by the beach.

When the company jet landed on the island the next day, out master told both Karl and I that we were going with him to the airstrip. He ordered us both to just put on a pair of tennis shoes. We were told to get in the back of the car and our master drove us out to the airstrip.

The pilots were waiting for us as we drove up to the airstrip. When Karl and I got out of the car our master ordered us to get the pilot's bags and some supplies out of the plane's cargo compartment. We quickly put the bags and boxes of supplies in the trunk of the car and got in the back seat. All the way to the guest house the pilots would occasionally turn around to look at us sitting naked in the back seat. They looked really hungry and I and Karl were going to be their main course. The attention that the pilots were giving us had an affect on us, our cocks were getting hard just thinking about balling the pilots again.

When we drove up to the main house Karl and I were told to unload the supplies and to put them in the house. As we took the supplies out of the trunk our master gave the car keys to Chuck and told him to, "Have fun with my boys and be sure to pick me up at 8:00 a.m. the next morning."

When Karl and I were done putting the supplies in the house we walked down to the car. The knowledge that we were going to service the pilots had both of our cocks hard and throbbing all the way down to the car.

When we got into the back seat of the car Chuck started the engine, but before we left both John and Chuck turned around and looked at us sitting naked in the back seat with roaring hardons. They both smiled and said, "Well, the boys belong to us tonight and they look really horny. We will have to really get a lot of use out of them tonight."

The trip to the beach house only took 5 minutes. When we got out of the car both Karl and I stood submissively next to the car. We waited for our one night masters to tell us what they wanted us to do. We were both a little startled when each of the pilots grabbed one of us by the hair on our heads and started to make out with us. After a few minutes of kissing John said, "Stop acting so rigid boys, we want to get down to some one on one as a starter. Do you two know how to make out or not?" We both just smiled and put our arms around the shoulders of the two pilots and we started to madly make out with them.

This little make out session went on for the next 15 minutes and it had my cock throbbing hard against my stomach.

After our make out session the pilots ordered us both to follow them into the beach house. When we got to the living room we were told to take off our tennis shoes and kneel submissively on the floor. While we knelt on the floor the pilots disappeared into one of the bedrooms.

In no time at all, two sets of bare feet were standing in front of us. "Well Chuck, which one of the boys do you want to fuck? I'll take Karl this time. I fucked Jimmy last time." Chuck ordered Karl to get to his feet and follow him. They both left the room leaving me silently kneeling on the floor. I waited for several minutes as John just sat down in a chair and said nothing. Suddenly, the sounds of moaning could be heard. Chuck had started to fuck Karl.

John suddenly yelled, "Fuck him good Chuck!" As I listened to the sounds of Chuck royally fucking Karl I was getting hornier and hornier. I started to think over and over again, please use me Sir please use me Sir! Finally, John said, "Are you getting really horny boy?" "Yes Sir!" "Well Boy I want you really hornier. You work best when you are super horny. Now get over here and licked my feet Boy." "Yes Sir!" I crawled over to John and I started to eagerly lick his feet. John liked the feel of my warm, wet tongue on his feet and he started to moan and squirm. After a few minutes of licking, John stopped me and than he put his hands under my armpits and lifted me on to my feet, put his arms around my shoulders and gave a long deep kiss on the lips. We made out again for about 10 minutes. I was soon turned on that I had to squeeze the head of my dick to stop from cumming.

I soon learned that John was not done with his little surprises. As John finished making out with me he looked deep into my eyes and than grabbed me by the shoulders. He than led me backwards and sat me down on the sofa. He kissed me one more time and than he started to kiss and lick his way down my naked body until he was licking my balls and stroking my cock. This at first startled me a little. I had been trained to give pleasure not receive it and what John was doing had me very confused. But my master had told me to please the pilots in any way that they wanted, so I guess what John was doing to me was alright.

I just continued to squirm and moan as John licked his way up my throbbing cock and start to slowly suck me off. As I started to build up to climax I couldn't help but think was it right for a master, even a temporary master, to suck a slave's cock. Than I started to wildly squirm and moan as I got close to cumming and I said, "Suck me master, suck me!"

As my body tensed up and I loudly moaned one more time I shot a big load down John's throat. He swallowed every drop and than he licked my big cock clean and than he lifted up his head and looked at me and smiled. "Well slave boy have I freaked you out yet?" "Yes Sir. But what I think doesn't matter. I am here to serve and please you Sir!"

"Good Boy and now for the main event of the evening." John pulled me to my feet and grabbed the back of my neck and led me into the second bed room. He pulled back the covers and than threw a pillow on the middle of the bed. "Now Boy it's time that I fucked that pretty ass of yours for a few hours."

John wasn't kidding about fucking me for a few hours. I had the pleasure of John's big cock up my ass for the next 3 hours. He shot a load up my ass 3 times before he was though with me for the night. That night I slept naked against John's warm body. Early the next morning, just after the sun had risen, John fucked me again for another hour. I started to think that John's middle name must be rabbit. Not that I was complaining.

When the pilots took off to take our master to the plane Karl and I were left to clean up the guest house. From the moment the pilots left Karl's personality changed. Since our master was gone for a few weeks, our master had put Karl in charge on the island. Karl was not the top boy any more, for the next few weeks he was my master. The slave brother relationship that I had worked so hard to establish for the last 6 months was now on hold. Karl owned me and he was going to really show me who was boss.

After letting me do most of the cleaning in the guest house Karl and I put on our tennis shoes and walked back to the house. The weather was already hot and humid. By the time we got to the main house our naked bodies were covered with sweat. Just after I followed Karl into the main house he told me to stand at attention, as he started to take off his cock ring. The silver ring on the end of his cock was a symbol of his slavery. After putting his cock ring on a counter in the kitchen he walked over to me, looked into my eyes and smiled, just as he grabbed my balls and squeezed them. My body squirmed and I thought, "Oh god he is going to castrate me."

Karl released my balls, but my body remained tense. I did not know what Karl had planned for me. Was he going to cut off my balls? He was my master. If he wanted to castrate me I would have no choice. I started to mentally repeat, I am a slave and I existed only to serve and please my master and Karl is my master. I am a slave…

My body shook and I started to breathe harder as Karl walked around me inspecting my body. He did not say a word for several minutes. Finally Karl stood in front of me and smiled. "Boy, get down on your knees." Yes Sir!" I dropped to my knees and submissively waited. "Now Boy, look at my balls." I looked up to see Karl stroking his cock and his balls moving up and down. "O.K. slave lick my balls." "Yes Sir!" As my warm, wet tongue hit his balls his body started to squirm. He liked the feel of someone licking his slave balls.

After getting Karl's balls completely wet I was order to suck his cock. I ran my tongue up the shaft of his throbbing cock and I started to play with his the head of his cock with my tongue for a minute before I deep throated his big cock right down to his hair. As

I continued to suck his cock his body shook and he moaned. He was really horny and it only took a few minutes for my warm and wet mouth to get him off. His big cock started to swell and he pumped a big load down my eager throat.

After Karl's big cock started to go limp I licked the last of his cum off of his cock and than I said, "Thank you Sir!" Karl looked pleased with me. My blow job and my submissive attitude had shown Karl that I had accepted him as my master. Karl ordered me to kneel and not to move. As he walked up the stairs to the second floor I smiled. I started to hope that my new master would want to fuck me tonight.

The rest of the day Karl had me do all of the house chores. When I did not have any duties to perform he had me kneel and remain silent for hours at a time. I now knew that Karl was going to get a lot of work out of me.

When evening came Karl came down the stairs wearing casual clothes. I looked at him and froze I had never seen Karl wearing clothes, even if it was only a tank top and some walking shorts. As Karl sat down at the table he told me to serve the dinner and I quickly obeyed. As Karl ate his dinner as I knelt naked by his chair. Every once in a while he would run his fingers though my hair or down my back and say, "God Boy."

That night I sat at his feet as Karl watched our master's big screen T.V. Later that night I followed Karl up to the master bedroom he was in the mood for a little fucking. Karl was quiet a stud, he fucked me twice that night and in the morning he fucked me again. It seemed that Karl was hornier than hell and he was sort of living out some sort of domination fantasy. During the next 3 weeks Karl fucked me several times a day, at any time and any place. He fucked me on the kitchen floor, on the stairs, bent over the back of the living room sofa, in the hallway leaning against the wall and in the shower. Karl owned my ass and he made good use of it when ever he felt like it.

It was interesting having Karl as my master for three weeks.

I like sucking cock and getting fucked and I was more than glad that Karl kept giving me his cock during our master's absence. I learned a lot more about Karl and his cock than I ever knew before. But, when our master came back we were back to being slave brothers kneeling naked at our master's feet.

Chapter 11:

VISITORS

It has been two years since my master bought me as his property. I have spent the past two years getting adjusted to my life as a slave on my master's island. I am now completely content with my station in life. I am my master's property and my whole life is serving his needs.

I now lead the life of a well-trained and devoted slave. I care for my master's needs and he takes care of me. I have no worries like average people. I have no money problems, I do not have to worry about taxes, having a career, paying the rent, owning and protecting personal property, or buying food. My master provides what I need. I only have one job in life and that is serving and pleasing my master.

My life as a slave has become very simple. All my material and sexual needs are taken care of. I live in a wealthy man's house and I always have enough to eat. My sexual needs are taken care of by my master, Karl and the two company pilots that service the island. For the first time in my life I feel content and safe. The reasons that I had in the past for fearing enslavement have disappeared. I do not relate to my former life at all any more. While I can say that my body is enslaved my mind still remains partially free. Mentally I have not completely given in completely to the control of my master. The thought of becoming, mentally and physically, a total slave still scares me.

My master is very pleased with the way that I have adjusted to being his property. He is not only my master, he has become my mentor and at times he treats me like more of a son than a slave. My master has told me that I am one of those rare people who is a natural born slave. He said, "Boy you were born to please men and to be a master's property. Your fate in life was to be a man's slave." What my master said would go a long way in explaining why I felt that going to Paris was part of my fate in life. Paris and Carlos led me into slavery. My master understands me. I feel very lucky to have such a man in my life.

But, like most ideal ways of life my life was about to run into a little strange weather with the arrival on the island of three different visitors, my master's brother Frank, a lady named Grace and Mr. Bronson.

It started just after our morning run. Our master, Karl and I had run over 3 miles and were just entering the main house when my master got a phone call. Karl and I were ordered to kneel on the living room floor as our master took the call. As beads of sweat run down our naked bodies we silently waited for the return of our master.

When our master returned about 15 minutes later he announced that his brother Frank was flying to the island tomorrow morning and we were told to get the guest house ready for my master's brother and his two aides.

I didn't know what to think. My master usually didn't allow visitors to his island and I didn't know that he had a brother. Karl on the other hand acted very nervous.

After Karl and I had rested up a little we started to jog down to the guest house. I knew that something was bothering Karl but it was not my place to ask him what it was. Karl started to tell me what was on his mind just after we started to jog down to the guest house. "Well Jimmy you are about to meet the black sheep of the family. His name is Frank, but I just call him Satan." "Karl what do you mean?" Karl looked very serious. "Frank is our master's business partner. Our master is the CEO of the corporation and Frank is the President." Karl remained silent for a while he was thinking about what to say. "Be ready to catch hell when Frank and his two aides are here. He hates gays and his aides are just like him. Frank puts up with our master's life style but not with his slaves. Just remember to stay out of his way and that goes for those two goons he calls aides."

My master's brother arrived early the next morning. Our master made some changes on the island to try to avoid trouble. Karl and I were told to put on casual clothes while our master's brother was on the island and Meg and Lacy were told to stay away from the main house during the time that our master's brother was here.

Karl told me later that the reason that Meg and lacy were told to stay away was that during the brother's last visit, three years ago, Lacy got so mad at our master's brother that she said that she was going to shot his bigoted ass. All of which sounded like a good reason to keep Lacy and our visitors apart.

As Karl drove our master and me out to the airstrip I kept having doubts about the whole idea of dealing with fag hating bigots again. I had hoped that I had left all that kind of hatred behind in Indiana. My arms shock a little. I didn't know if I could handle those fears from my childhood again. As my arms stopped shaking I thought maybe it won't be all that bad. Maybe in the last 3 years my master's brother has changed.

Our master had both Karl and me put on gym sweats. He wanted us to wear clothes while his brother was on the island.

When we drove up to the airstrip the plane's crew were was already unloading the plane. The plane was not the corporate jet that usually flew to the island and the pilots were two men that I had never seen before. While both Karl and I leaned against the car our master went over to greet his brother. The brother said, "How are you doing big brother?" He smiled and hugged our master. I looked at the two brothers and thought that the brother looked happy, maybe there won't be any trouble on this trip to the island.

My master's brother looked a lot like him except for the fact that he had darker hair and quiet a gut on him. Unlike our master his brother did not keep care of himself. The two aides I noticed were both carrying guns. They also both had red hair and stocky builds. The two aides looked like they were members of the Irish Mafia.

Our master ordered Karl and I to put his visitors bags and the new supplies in the trunk. Karl and I tried to avoid looking at the visitors and the visitors seem to avoid eye contact with us. This arrangement did not last long. After the bags and supplies were loaded into the trunk our master's brother looked at Karl and me and said, "Hey Rick I do not want to have those two faggots of your ride with us. Just looking at them makes my skin crawl."

I suppose for the sake of avoiding trouble, or for business reasons our master told us to jog back to the main house. Our master than drove the visitors to the guest house. As the care disappeared into the distance I looked at Karl. The pained expression on his face said it all. We were in for a bumpy ride.

It only took us a half hour to jog back to the main house. Our master's car was already parked in front. When we walked into the house we were relieved to see that our visitors were not in the house. Our master told us to get the house ready for dinner party. We were to have things ready by 7:00 p.m. Our master left us alone to work on the dinner while he when upstairs to work in his computer room.

When the visitors arrived for dinner I did not know what to expect. Karl did not hold out much hope for a quiet evening. "Hell, last time Frank was here for a formal dinner he got mad and he threw a gravy desk at me." As the dinner quests arrived all I could do was hope for the best.

When the dinner quests were seated Karl looked at the clock in the kitchen. "I say it will be no more than 5 minutes before Frank says something offensive." I just smiled and started to carry the main dish, baked ham, into the dining room. As I was putting down the dish Frank started up, "Well, I see you bought yourself another faggot. I guess you into pretty boy faggots now."

Our master did not like his brother's comment. "Frank! I told you to watch your mouth while you are on my island. Remember, I can still kick your big ass just like when we were kids." "O.K. O.K. I'll lay off the faggot talk."

The rest of the dinner went alright. Frank mined his manners and his aides kept quiet too. Karl and I were soon to learn that Frank had said that he would be a good boy not his aides. When dinner was over and my master and his brother went upstairs to discuss business the two aides sat down in the living room to watch T.V. Well, at least Karl and I hoped they would just watch T.V.

The aides stayed put for about an hour as Karl and I cleaned up after the dinner. Than during one intermission one of the aides yelled at Karl. "Hay bald headed faggot get me a beer." Karl gave the guy a cold stare and said nothing. "Hay you faggot, I told you to get me a beer." This time Karl said something. "The beers are in the fridge help yourself." The aides face turned red with rage and he blotted out of his chair and headed for the kitchen. Before I could warn Karl the guy was yelling in his face. "You stupid little faggot when I tell you to do something you do it, do you hear me faggot!" Karl just turned and looked directly into his eyes and said, "I work for my master not you. Get your own fucking beer."

I thought that the guy was going to hit Karl when I heard someone coming in a hurry down the stairs. A familiar voice yelled, "What hell is going on down here?" It was my master and he was not in a good mood. When he got to the kitchen he told the aide to back off now! Both the aides looked startled as my master said, "You two just wore out your welcome. Take a hike." The aides did not say a thing they just left.

After the aides were gone our master looked at Karl and me and said, "Sorry about that boys some people lack social graces." After our master left to go back upstairs I started to laugh a little. Karl looked at me like I was a little crazy and said, "What is there to laugh about Boy?" "Oh I was just thinking to bad that redneck didn't jump on you, you would have beaten the shit out of him." Karl just laughed. "Yes, he is in pretty bad shape isn't he." It was nice to be able to laugh about the whole thing but we still knew that those two goons could be dangerous.

Our master's brother only stayed on the island for another day. After they were gone we all went back to our normal routine. That is until Grace came to visit and my life took a very odd turn.

It all started with a photo and a lab test. About 6 months after my master's brother and his friends left, my master had a new assignment for me. My master showed up with a camera and what looked like a medical jar with some sort of liquid in it. After he had taken about 50 pictures of me in the nude and with clothes on, my master told me that he wanted to take a lab sample of my cum. He told me that it would be sent to a lab to find out how fertile I was. Nothing more was said and it was not my place to ask. My cum belonged to my master and he could do with it as he pleased. After shooting my load in a jar I went back to doing my house duties and I forgot about the whole thing.

Three months later the company jet arrived on the island and this time only my master went out to meet it. On this trip the plane was not going to stay over night, it was to leave for Hawaii right after stopping on the island. Both Karl and I were a little sad that we would not be entertaining Chuck and John on this trip..

While I was cleaning part of the kitchen I heard my master's car return from the airstrip. But this time something was not the same. I could hear two voices and one was that of a woman. I quickly looked out the kitchen window to see my master with a very pretty young blond lady of about 28 years of age. I was a little startled, not because I was naked, but because I had never seen nor heard of a woman visiting the island.

May master walked into the kitchen with the strange woman right behind him. He told me to get up. He wanted to introduce me to his cousin Grace. "Grace this is Jimmy the young man that I told you about." The pretty blond lady just remained silent while she was looking over my naked body. She smiled and said, "It is good to meet you Jimmy."

My master put his arm around my shoulders and said, "He's a find looking young stud isn't he Grace?" "Yes, Richard he looks better in person than in those photos that you sent me. May I have a closer look?" "Go ahead Grace inspect him." The woman started to walk around me visually inspecting my naked body. She made several sounds that sounded like she approved of what he was looking at. I smiled, she seems to like me and that will please my master.

After her inspection, she said a few things to my master that I couldn't hear I expected her to physically inspect me next. But I was wrong. Instead of a physical inspection my master's cousin walked over to her a small suitcase and she took out a folder. She than asked my master, "Can I interview him in private?" "Sure Grace you can use the living room I will be upstairs if you need me. After telling me to do what ever his cousin wanted me to do, my master left and went upstairs.

I was now standing completely naked in front of a very well dressed and pretty young lady. The lady looked over my body one more time and smiled. "Young man my name is Grace would you please follow me into the living room." "Yes Miss." Grace sat in one of the single chairs and than she asked me to kneel on the carpet in front of her. I knelt down and I assumed a submissive posture. But it seems she did not want me to be submissive.

"Jimmy please sit up and put your hands on your knees and look at me." "Yes Miss." As I assumed new posture I could see that

Grace was staring at my eyes, than she smiled and broke eye contact and started to look though her folder.

"Well Jimmy my file on you says that you grew up in Indiana and your parents died when you were 10 years old. Is that right Jimmy?" "Yes Miss." "Jimmy tell me about your parents." "Yes Miss. My parents were teachers. My father was a professor and my mother was a high school teacher. I still miss them." Grace smiled and turned a page in her folder. "Jimmy your high school records show that you got straight A's. Why didn't you go to college?" "I thought about it but I didn't have any money and I had other interests that I wanted to look into." Grace looked at me and smiled. "Yes, I can see that you had some interesting interests to look into. "Were you happy in high school?" "No Miss, I hated high school and the whole fag hating town that I lived in."

Grace took out a note pad and the discussion took a completely different turn. "Jimmy did your family have any physical or mental problems?" "No Miss, there was no such problems that I knew of. My family was just my parents and me and some distant relatives. None of whom had any physical or mental problems it seems." "Jimmy have you ever had sexual relations with a girl?" "Yes Miss, I played around with three girls in high school. There were not many gay guys in my high school." "Why did you have sex with these girls?" "They were my friends and they seemed to like guys who were super hung." "Did you like fucking your girl friends?" "It was alright, but I prefer guys." That will be all for now Jimmy. You can go back to your job. I want to talk with your master." That was the end of the interview, but not the end of Grace's interest in me.

After I had finished my kitchen work on knelt down next to the front door and waited for my master to have another job for me. In just about 15 minutes my master came down the stairs and he told me to get up and to follow him out to the front porch. When we were outside my master asked me what I thought of his cousin Grace. I told him she was a nice and very pretty young lady. "Will Boy she thinks you are a very interesting young man. In fact she thinks you are perfect for the job." My master now told me that I could speak freely and I asked him what job he meant. "My cousin wants to be a single mom and she has picked you to be her stud. I have already volunteered your services. Do you have a problem with being a stud?" "No Sir, if that is what you want Sir!" My master smiled at me and than he patted me on the back and we when back into the house.

When we got back into the house my master ordered me to kneel on the floor and to wait he was going to talk to Grace. As my master left the room I smiled. My master had patted me on the back. That meant that he was super proud of me and that made me very happy.

A few minutes my master came back into the room with Grace. I was told to get up and face my master and Grace. He told me that, "Boy for the next 3 weeks you belong to my cousin Grace. You job is to have sex with her as offer as she wants. You are her stud and I expect a baby out of this mating. You understand boy!" Like a prized stallion I was to be used for breeding purposes. Grace looked a little uptight about how direct and forceful my master had been. After my master left she told me to put on some shoes, we were going for a walk on the beach.

We walked on the beach and talked about Grace's need to be a mother and why she had picked me be her stud. I felt honored to have been picked. I had never really thought about being a father before, but if it was what my master wanted and it would please Grace than it was alright with me. As if I had any real say in the matter.

The weather on the beach was hot and humid and by the time Grace and I got back to the house I had beads of sweat running down my naked body. This did not seem to bother Grace it seemed to actually turn her on. Grace told me to take off my tennis shoes and to follow her upstairs.

As we entered one of the guest bedrooms Grace told me pull back the covers and to sit down on the side of the bed and than she disappeared into the bathroom. A few minutes later she walked into the room completely naked, with a hungry look on her face. I just stared at her naked body for a moment. Grace was one good looking and sexy lady with clothes on or without. She stood for a moment only a few feet from me and visually inspected my sweat covered naked body. Suddenly, she got on her knees and she started to lick my cock, up one side and down the other. The feel of her warm, wet tongue on my cock had me hard in no time.

Grace now started to stoke my big cock as she licked my balls. The sensation had me squirming in my chair. After she finished with my balls she went down on me and started to slowly suck my cock. As she deep throated my cock my whole body started to shake. God, she was good.

After several minutes of sucking my cock she started to lick her way up my stomach and chest, while she stroked my cock, until she was kissing me on the lips. She suddenly stopped kissing me and she stood up with my cock still in her hand. She looked over my sweat covered body and smiled just before she mounted my throbbing hard cock. I moaned and my body shook as my big cock slid deep into her warm pussy. She leaned forward and put her hands on my shoulders as she started to ride my cock. I had not cum in almost three weeks and it took only a few minutes for me to shot a big load into Grace. But this did not stop Grace she just kept riding my still hard cock until her eyes glazed over and her body tensed up as she came.

As she moved off of my cock she rolled over on her side on the bed and than she told me to get up next to her. She gave me a long deep kiss and than she ran her hand over my bare chest, looked into my eyes and smiled. "You know for a gay man you are quiet a good fuck. I am going to get a lot of work out of you stud boy the next 3 weeks." With that she put her head down on my chest and we slept for the next hour.

Grace said that she would get a lot of work out of me and she did. Grace was a good teacher. In no more than a week I was fucking her 2 or 3 times a day just like a straight guy. I suppose I was alright in bed, Grace always seemed content with my performance.

While I saw fucking Grace as just another job Karl thought the whole idea was a good opportunity to make fun of me. Sometimes when I was working with him he would make comments like, "Well stud Boy eat any pussy today." I didn't respond to his teasing. Karl was my boss and when our master was gone he was my master, so I thought it was best to just let Karl have his fun.

Grace stayed three weeks and when she left I was able to get back to a life style that I actually enjoyed, being my master's property. My master seemed very proud of me. For a few weeks he called me his stud boy and he rewarded me by letting me have his cock twice a day and letting me sleep with him for a week. My master was happy with my performance, as was Grace and that was all that mattered to me.

Two months after Grace had left the island my master told me that Grace was expecting. I smiled for several days after I heard the news, "God damn, I was going to be a father. Talk about unexpected events in my life. But of coarse my whole life has been one big unexpected event after another.

The following six months was pure slave heaven for me. I just kept care of my master and his house. To me this was the perfect life. I had no worries and I felt safe and content. But, everybody knows that good things don't last.

After the mental and verbal abuse of our master's brother and my being used for stud service, the arrival of Mr. Bronson on the island was a welcome relief, well at first I thought it would be.

Mr. Bronson arrived on his own personal jet. Our master went out to the airstrip by himself to pick him up. Karl told me that Mr. Bronson is a very rich and powerful man and a close friend of our master's. It seems that Mr. Bronson is also a very strict slave master who owns two slaves. According to Karl one is an Amerasian stud and the other is a blond haired German stud. Both slaves are in their twenties, extremely good-looking, well-built, and hung." Both of Mr. Bronson's slaves worship their master.

Karl told me, "Jimmy, get ready for a wild ride. Our master has assigned you to serve Mr. Bronson's needs while he is on the island." I didn't know what to say, I was worried that I wouldn't measure up to Mr. Bronson's standards.

When our master got back from the airstrip, both Karl and I were kneeling naked on the front porch. Our master quickly ordered us both to get Mr. Bronson's bags from the truck of the car. As I passed Mr. Bronson, with my head bowed, I could feel his eyes inspecting my naked body.

As Karl and I finished putting away Mr. Bronson's clothes into the closet and drawers of the quest bedroom we were summoned to the living room. We quickly ran down the stairs and submissively kneeled on the living room floor.

"Well Bill, I see that you have a new slave. Can I have permission to inspect him?" "You can do more than just permission to inspect him Richard, he is your property while you are my quest." "Thank you, I will make good use of him." A mild chill passed through my body as Mr. Bronson walked over and stood in front of me.

"Get up Boy!" I said, "Yes, Sir" as I got to my feet and stood submissively in front of Mr. Bronson. "Look at me Boy!" "Yes, Sir," now I stood, looking directly into Mr. Bronson's very stern and rather cold eyes. I could sense right away that this was a man nobody should mess with. While his physical presence was intimidating there was something very sexually attractive about this manner. He had a very strong, animalistic sex appeal.

"Now Boy, in the next few weeks I am going to find out who you really are. I am going to be affectionate." He leaned forward and gave me a long slow kiss and than backed off and looked at me directly in my eyes. "And I will be abusive." He now grabbed and twisted both of my nipples until my body squirmed. He said, "I will also, be very caring." He now stroked the hair on the back of my head, as he looked into my eyes and smiled. "And at times very cruel," as he squeezed by balls so hard I almost fainted.

He now backed away from my still trembling body. "Boy, I am going to find out who you really are. I am going to find out things that even you do not know about yourself."

"Now Boy, go up to my room and kneel on the floor next to the bedroom door." "Yes Sir!"

It was a good half hour before my new master came up the stairs. He at first did not pay any attention to me. He just walked into the room and shut the door behind him, leaving me kneeling naked on the hallway floor. I hear him undress and lie down on the bed. For the next two hours I hear nothing, but the slight sounds of my breathing and at times people walking and talking down stairs. I used my breathing exercises to relax my body as I waited for my master to have a need for me.

Finally, I heard my master get up and walk around his room. Suddenly, the door opened and two bare feet appeared in front of me followed by the feeling of a hand grabbing the hair on the back of my head, as I was forcibly yanked to my feet, led into the room, and thrown face first on to the bed.

As quickly as I regained my senses I felt two hands part my ass checks, following by the sudden thrust of a big greased cock, deep into my ass. My whole body tensed up and I grit my teeth as my master started to, caringly and violently, fuck me for the next hour or so, until he had shot his load up my ass four times. It seemed to me at the time that this was my new master's way of claiming his new property.

I really enjoyed taking a shower with my master. I had, up to this point, no real chance to see what he looked like. As I soaped down his body I took mental inventory of his physical assets. He was a good looking man, of about 36 years of age, with dark hair and piercing eyes. He stood about 6'2" tall and he had a very muscular, well-defined and almost hairless body. He weighed over 200 pounds and his beautiful man cock must have been about 9 plus inches. I felt lucky to have had the chance to please such a stud.

After helping to prepare and serve dinner I sat naked at my master's feet the rest of the evening, while he talked to my real master and they watched T.V. Than my master was good to me he allowed me to sleep with him. I slept very contently that night.

The next morning I had the pleasure of sucking off my still horny master. His big load tasted so good that I started eagerly look forward to the next time I could drain his cock.

After doing our usual early morning jog on the beach we returned to the house and my master told me to not shower and to just take off my gym shoes and kneel on the front porch. The early morning heat caused droplets of sweat to form all over my naked body.

It seems that my master had a list of questions he wanted me to answer. "Boy, serving your master properly, means not making any mistakes. As you will learn mistakes are costly. He than walked over a chair and picked up a cat of nine tails whip. As he walked over to me he dragged the tails of the whip on the ground. Suddenly, I felt the whip tails mildly caress my bare back. My body started to tense up.

"Boy I am going to go over your life with your help and find out the mistakes that you have made. You will be punished for these mistakes and you can learn from them and let them go.

The next two days were spent on retracing my life and inspecting the mistakes that I had made. Many of my mistakes I had not realized were errors in my life until my master pointed them out and told me what I should have do. The whippings hurt, but the whole head trip actually worked and I started to plan my actions, in the service of my master; in advance. I make fewer mistakes. My master rewarded me with his cock and letting me sleep with him, a pleasure that I started to crave.

The three weeks that Mr. Bronson spent as my master's guest went much to fast. He had taken me to a whole new level of submission. I found that I felt safe and very content with my life under his domination and part of me was sorry to see him leave. At the same time his way of total control sort of scared the rest of me. I intend to return to regular every day life after my slavery contract was up and the memory of being owned by Mr. Bronson was getting to be like trying to get rid of a drug habit. Mr. Bronson could really get inside a slaves head. It has started to weigh on my mind. I knew in the back of my mind that serving Mr. Bronson for a long period of time would mean that mentally, as well as physically, I would become a total slave.

What Mr. Bronson said to me before he left did not help cure my mental conflict. He told me after inspecting my naked body one last time, "Boy, I am starting to be impressed with you. Some day I intend to own your pretty slave ass and than I will make sure that you live up to your full potential as a man slave."

Hopefully, I will be able to get Mr. Bronson and the thought of being a man slave out of my system, before it takes over my mind and the slave in me becomes me.

Chapter 12:

BROTHER TROUBLE

It was late at night when the bad news arrived. My master was dead! He had been killed in a car accident in France. The news hit both Karl and me pretty hard. At first we didn't know what to say or think we just sat down and cried.

Our master was dead and the basis for our lives was gone. Both of us handled the news in our own way. Karl retreated to the master bedroom and he just rested on our master's bed for several hours. I just had to get out of the house for a while. I took a long walk down the beach. The feel of the cool night air on my naked body felt good.

When I got back to the house I started to look for Karl. I found him in an unexpected place. He was in our late master's office going though his safe. "What are you doing Karl?" Karl gave me a rather cold look. "Boy you have better realize the situation that we are in. Our master is dead and his brother will be arriving on the island within a few days. It is best that we get the hell out of here unless you want to end up dead." I knew that Karl was right. Our late master's brother hates the both of us and we are not safe on the island any more.

Karl handed me a pile of items from our master's safe and told me to put them on the office desk. After I put the pile down I had to ask him, "Karl how is it you know the combination to our master's safe?" "Boy our late master trusted me. I was his chief boy and his aide. He trusted me totally."

After Karl put several bags and a metal box on the desk we both started to look though the material. We soon found both of our passports and our slave files, the files that had our personal histories, our birth certificates and even our slave contracts. The lock box and the bags contained gold coins and American dollars. All in all, the safe contained about $40,000 in cash and at least that amount in gold coins.

Karl gave me my personal papers and half of all the cash and gold coins. We stashed the papers and money in two back packs and left them in the master bedroom. Now Karl turned to more pressing matters like how to get off the island. He e-mailed the two company pilots to see if they could fly in and get us off the island. We waited for an answer for several hours, but there was none. Karl began to look a little nervous.

"Well boy it will probably be several days before our late master's brother arrived, so we have a little time to play with. The pilots will contact us. I just know they will not let us down. It is best not to worry to much about it. We had better start to pack some clothes. We need to get ready to leave."

I did as Karl told me. In a strange sort of way he was now in charge of my life and he seemed to know what to do. After giving up on getting an e-mail from the pilots we both went to sleep in our late master's bed.

I woke up early the next morning, shortly after sunrise, to the feel of a warm breeze flowing over my naked body, as I and Karl began to slowly wake up. As Karl began to move and stretch his body he lifted his head off of my chest and looked into my eyes. "Well, good morning free boy." He than got up on his knees next to me in our former master's big bed and said, "Turn over free boy, you look like you could use a good strong, wake-up message." I did not say anything, I just smiled and rounded over on my stomach as Karl mounded my ass and began to message my shoulders and neck.

Karl was a creature of habit to the core and he could not just get rid of the routine that he had called his life, during his years of slavery on the island. Ever morning it had been his duty to message our master, just after he had woken up and he was still performing his duties. The message felt so good that I didn't even think about telling Karl that he did not have any duties anymore, he was now a free man.

As I enjoyed the feel of Karl's strong hands messaging every inch of my relaxed body, I slowly came to realize why Karl had volunteered to give me an expert message he really did not like the idea of being a free man. For the moment at least, I was his substitute master as he spent the next hour messaging my naked body, just before he went down on my throbbing hard cock and gave me a long slow blow job that had my body tensing and squirming several times before I finally shot a big load down Karl's thirsty throat.

It took Karl almost a half hour to suck me off. I was extremely horny, but I had trouble just letting go. I had been well trained to only cum when my master gave me permission and I not yet know how to act with out a master to tell me what to do. Freedom brings personal responsibility and I was a little scared of running my own life again, even in simple matters like getting off. After all, I was never really good at running my own life in the past.

After Karl was finish sucking me off he licked his way up my stomach and chest and gave me a light kiss, just before his body settled down on mine with his head on my chest. It was the same routine that he had followed so many times with our master and he seemed very content and relaxed as he rested his head on my chest.

As Karl went to sleep on my naked body and I began to relax, expecting to sleep one last time in my former master's bed, I heard the sound of a car driving up to the house. My eyes opened wide and shock Karl, waking him up, as I quickly got out of bed and ran over to the window, only to see something that startled me. My former master's jerk of a brother and his two bodyguards had arrived way earlier than we had expected.

I looked at Karl and said, "They are here already, what can we do? We can't let them find us here. You know what he is like." Karl got up and grabbed my shorts and shirt and threw them to me. Karl did not look as scared as I was, he seemed to know something. "Get dressed Randy, I have a plan, we'll be alright, trust me." Trust him, yes I will trust him, what choice did I have.

Just after we had gotten our clothes on we heard the sound of keys opening the front door. Karl motioned to me to pick up one of the backpacks in which we had packed our personal items and the valuables from the safe and to follow him. I expect to quickly follow down the back stairs and out the back door, but he ran over to the bookcase that was built into the wall and pulled a book out. The wall opened up. There was a staircase behind the bookcase. As we both entered this secret space and started to close the bookcase I could hear the sound of footsteps in the hall outside of our master's bedroom.

Both I and Karl sat down on the stairs and remained completely quiet, as several people entered the master bedroom. At first we could hear only the sounds of at least two people ransacking the room, as if they were looking for something or someone. Suddenly, someone can into the room and the sounds of searching stopped. "Well, did you find them?" It was the voice of my late master's brother. "No, but the bed is still warm, so they have not been gone long. They may still be in the house." "I want those two perverts found and taken care of. I don't want anyone in the business world to find out what was going on here. My brother had a good reputation and I intend to keep it that way. When you find my brother's little play things, cuff them and take them out deep into the jungle and dispose of them. Also, if those two dikes on still on the island waste the both of them. How you do it is up to you. You have the next week to find them. If you want to kill them slowly it's up to you, just make sure the remains will never be found, understand!" "Yes Sir, we understand."

"If you want to find me I will be in the basement, going though the contents of the safe room." The safe room is a fire proof security room in the basement. Family valuables and important papers are stored there.

After the brother left it sounded like the two bodyguards fixed themselves some drinks from the master bedroom mini-bar and sat down to discuss what they intended to do next.

"Well Fred, where do you think they are hiding?" "It's a small island we will find them with out much trouble." "Well than, sit down and have a drink." We could hear the sounds of the second man sitting down and of ice hitting the sides of a glass. The two bodyguards were making themselves at home.

"Well Fred, when we find those two queers, how do you think we should do them?" "I'm thinking of making it interesting, nothing fast like a bullet in the back of the head. Something more primitive would be entertaining." "What do you have in mind that might interest me?" "I'm thinking of something old fashion and very painful, impalement." "What do you mean?" "Well, when we find them we will strip and cuff the both of them. Then we will beat the crap out of them. After any real fight is kicked out of them we will lock them in the empty storage room and get ready to kill the two perverts in a very painful way."

"With the two boys safely locked-up we prepare to give them the ride of their lives that is as long as they stay alive. We will get two 6 foot by 3 inch fence posts, an ax and a slough hammer from the barn and than we will find a spot in the jungle that no one will ever visit. When we have found the right spot it is only a matter of using the ax to sharpen the ends of the posts before we pound them about 2 feet into the ground and than sharpening the exposed end."

"When we get back to the house we just have to pick up a can of Crisco and go collect the gay boys, gag and blindfold them and than escort them out to site. After we grease the posts and mount the boys we can sit down and watch the fun. Be sure to bring some beers, we will be there for a few hours.

"Well Fred, won't they freak when they start sliding down the poles. Yes, and just to make it more interesting we will take their gags and blindfolds off. Than they can scream all they want no one will hear them. It will be interesting to watch them squirm and scream in acute pain as they slowly slid down the posts." They both laughed and than started to act like killing us would be some type of crude joke. "This will be the first time either of these boys has been fucked by a fence post. Do you thing the pretty boy will get a hard on as he slides down the post. I have heard that he likes really big ones."

"Tell me Fred, you got this idea from your tour in Nam didn't you?" The two just laughed again. "Yes, I was in Army Intelligence and torturing captured Viet Cong was one of my jobs. Impalement was a great way to get information from a prisoner. I remember how I once impaled two Charlie's on stakes. The pain was unbearable and both of them wanted to die fast. That was my angle. If they gave me the information that I wanted on hidden arms, I would kill them fast. They both tried giving me phony information at first and I quickly had it checked out. As the hours pasted and the pain became more acute they started to talk. With in just a few hours they both given me the locations of the arms sites and we cleaned them out."

"So, did you shot them?" "Hell no, I let the two commie bastards ride their poles. One died in about three hours. The pole cut its way through him and came out his chest before he finally died. The other gook was a tough little bastard he lasted a full three days. After all that I had been through in Nam I really enjoyed seeing those two gooks suffer."

"You know Fred you are a real mean mother fucker." They both started to laugh again.

"Mean, why do you get off on calling me mean. Remember, you're the guy who took three days once to torture and kill that one guy, using only a pair of pliers and a blow touch."

"It was nothing personal the boss wanted him done that way. If it were left up to me I just would have shot him in the head."

The thought of being impaled on a greased fence post and left to slowly die by these two bastards was beginning to get to me. I just know that this was not the way that I wanted my life to end. My body began to shake a little. But, my survival instinct was strong and I remained silent.

After we stake the two Faggots we will go back to the house and help the boss. The next day we go back out to the site to bury the bodies. If any of the boys are still alive you can put a bullet in his head. After we bury the bodies in that jungle no one will ever find the remains."

"O.K. man lets find those two bastards and stake their asses." With that statement the two bodyguards left the room and Karl motioned for me to quietly follow him down the stairs and into a underground tunnel that I never know existed.

The tunnel came out several hundred feet from the house. We could still hear the sounds of the bodyguards searching the house and yelling at each other.

As both I and Karl disappeared into the surrounding jungle I began to feel a little more at ease, at least for the moment. We were out of sight of the house, but we were still on the island and as long as we were we would not be safe.

For the next several hours both I and Karl followed a small path through the jungle until we started to climb the mountains that separated the two sides of the island. Half way over the mountains we ran into something unexpected. As I climbed to the top of a small ridge I found myself face to face with the business end of a rifle. I froze.

"Well, if it isn't Jimmy and Karl, we are glad to see that you two are still alive." It was Meg and her girlfriend. I relax and Meg put the rifle down and hugged me and Karl.

"Boys, it is good to see that those bastards haven't got you yet." I just smiled and said, "How did you two know about the brother and his goons arriving on the island early?" "We saw the jet come into the airstrip the quiet way. They didn't fly over the main house as visitors usually do they came in flying low from the opposite direction. We were out fishing when they flew in and we decided to come over the mountains and see if we could get you two out of harms way."

Both I and Karl told the girls about what our master's jerk of a brother had planned for all of us. The girls looked shocked and quickly told us to follow them we were going to leave the island as soon as possible.

Meg and Lacy had already prepared their 42 foot sailboat for a long trip. It only took us an extra half hour to grab a few extra items before we set sail for Hawaii and what was an uncertain future for me.

After getting under way I went below and sat on the floor of the main cabin with my back against the wall and I started to shake. The fear was still with me. The thought that

we had almost been caught by those bodyguards made me start to cry. Only about 30 seconds had separated us from a very painful death. That is the amount of time between the secret bookcase door closing and the moment the two bodyguards walked into the master bedroom. Karl came down the stairs and sat down next to me and put his arm around me. "We are safe now. You have nothing to fear."

Chapter 13:

RETURN TO PARIS

It took several weeks for the four of us to reach Hawaii. Seeing the island of Oahu appear on horizon was a big thrill for all of us. Both Karl and I bid farewell to Meg and Lacy at the airport. Meg and Lacy were going to set sail for South America and Karl and I were going to fly to Europe. I was going back to Paris to try to find Carlos and Karl was going to Germany to see his family.

On the long flight to Paris, I decided to read my slave file. All of these years I had not even known that this file existed let alone know what was in it. My history file was about an inch thick and it was surprisingly complete. It had about every detail about my life from birth to the time that I was sold as a slave. It even had the names of the porn films that I had made. It also, had documents such as my birth certificate and my California driver's license.

The file also had my slave contract. I had never really read the whole document, only the first page. As I started to read the contract I saw nothing unexpected. The first page was the same as I remembered. I had sold myself into slavery for a period of five years. The first two pages were a basic slave contract but the last page was something that I didn't expect. This page had a section that I was not told about. It gave my master the right to enslave me for life, if he saw a need for it.

I had signed all three pages and unknowingly had given my master the right to enslave me for life. The page had a space for my master to sign if he had decided to keep me for more than the regular five years. My master had signed the page. The page was dated only 6 months ago.

I didn't know what to think. I was both shocked and pleased. I was shocked that I had been sold for life and at the same time I felt pleased that the master that I worshiped wanted to keep me.

My master had no intention of ever setting me free as I had been led to believe, he was going to keep me as a slave, on his island, for the rest of my life. I thought that I should be shocked to learn that I had been sold for life, but I wasn't. Maybe, it was my fate to be a slave for the rest of my life. I had been very content with my life as my master's slave. But now my fate had suddenly changed. I was now a free man again and I didn't know if I could handle this new found freedom. Maybe, my late master did know what was best for me.

When I arrived in Paris, I expected to feel somewhat at home, since I had lived in Paris with Carlos for six months. But instead I felt very uneasy. Paris seemed even more strange and foreign than the first day that I saw it. Maybe, it was the training that I had gone through, or the three years on the island. I just knew that I was not the same young man that I was the first time that I had arrived in Paris. I just knew that something was not right.

I checked into the same small hotel that I lived in when I first came to Paris. After checking in with only the backpack that I brought from the island I realized that I needed more than one set of casual clothes. Shopping for clothes brought back some pleasant memories. I walked past the café that I had been sitting at when I first saw Carlos and I shopped in the same clothing stores that Carlos had taken me to.

By the time that I got back to my hotel I knew that I had to try to find Carlos. The thought of a long awaited reunion with Carlos had me in very high spirits.

I phoned Carlos the minute that I got back to my room. I dialed the phone number Carlos's townhouse and an old man answered the phone. He did not know of any one called Carlos. After hanging up the phone I felt very low for a moment. I could only think that maybe the number had been changed. Rather than go through the long hassle of trying to get the Paris phone system to look up Carlos's new number I decided to take a taxi over to the house that I had shared with Carlos.

All the way to the townhouse my heart half expected a tearful reunion with Carlos, while I also suspected that something was very wrong. After I knocked on the door a young woman opened the door. She told me in fairly good English that she had lived in the house for about three years and that she did not know anything of a man named Carlos.

My first efforts to find Carlos led to dead ends. Carlos's address and phone number were now useless and I didn't even have a picture of him. I had only one option left, to visit the few leather bars in Paris in the hopes of finding Carlos, or at least someone who knew him.

That night, I dressed in a daddy's boy outfit, tight jeans, tea shirt and tennis shoes and started to make the rounds of the bars that Carlos and I occasionally went too. The first bar was a bust, no Carlos and no one who seemed to know him. But, only minutes after entering the second bar, Carlos walked in. I was so shocked to see him again that I just sat in the crowded and dimly lit background and stared at him. Carlos was more muscular than when I had lived with him he had been hitting the gym. He was still the strikingly handsome man that I had fallen in love with.

While I in the background to uptight to say anything Carlos went up to a good looking, red haired, young man and started a conversation. Carlos was still the great talker and the young man seemed to be fascinated with him.

Looking at the way the young man was acting reminded me of the night that I met Carlos in this very same bar. Carlos was such a good looking, sexy, man of the world, that I just knew that I had to have him. Carlos on the other hand was probably looking me over to see how much he could sell me for as a slave. I was younger and my taste in men left a lot to be desired. But, even knowing what Carlos was really like, I still felt a great attraction to him. This fascination with Carlos that I still harbored scared me so much that my hands began to shack. I put my bottle of beer down and tried to concentrate on relaxing. It took about 10 minutes to calm my nerves.

The young man with Carlos was smiling and his eyes were fixed on Carlos all the time. He was buying every line that Carlos used on him. I just knew that I had to do something. I finally got up the nerve to walk over to stand in back of Carlos. I put my hand on his shoulder and said, "Hello Carlos." When Carlos turned around his face turned pale. He looked like he was in a state of shock. His eyes looked startled and his mouth dropped. I looked at him with a cold stare and said, "Well Carlos, aren't you glad to see me?

Carlos quickly regained his composure and said, "Who are you have we ever met before?" "Don't you remember me, I'm Jimmy?" "No, I never have known anyone named Jimmy. You must have me confused with someone else." With that statement, Carlos quickly left the bar. I didn't know what to say or do. Should I follow him and try to talk to him?

The young man that Carlos had been talking to looked at me like I had ruined a good thing for him. He just gave me a cold stare and walked off into the crowd not realizing that I may have just saved his life.

While I was trying to make up my mind on what to do next, if anything, someone tapped me on the shoulder. It was an older man in leather who said that he needed to talk to me about the man I called Carlos. He asked me to follow him outside and we walked out of the bar and across the street.

As I followed the man out of the bar I looked down the street. I could see Carlos he was only about a block down the street. A blond haired young man was walking not more than 10 paces behind him. At the time I didn't pay much attention to this fact.

The man than introduced himself, he was a Captain Foch, of the Paris Police Department and he was very interested in the man called Carlos. It seemed that Carlos had more than one name, many more. The police were investigating him for being engaged in running a slavery ring in North Africa. According to what the police had found, Carlos and his family were involved in a criminal organization. They recruit, train and sell young, good looking, male slaves for a secret organization that is run out of Morocco.

The policeman was only telling me what I already suspected. I had pretty well figured out that I had been conned into being a slave and that Carlos had not expected to every see me again.

The Captain took me down to a late night café and over some coffee we continued our conversation. He was very interested in what I had to tell him about what had happened to me. The policeman told me that I was very lucky to be alive. I was the only slave that the Hussien Organization had trained and sold who ever had returned alive. Hussien slaves were not supposed to come back after they were sold. Such slaves were either kept for life or they were killed.

The Captain brought me up to date on his investigation of the Hussien Organization. The Captain told me, "I have a man on the inside of the organization, but he will only give me certain types of information. He is not concerned about the basic organization. He is only interested in shutting down the Hussien Organization."

My informant has nothing against the way the basic organization is run. He sees it as nothing more than a well organized form of prostitution and he is not concerned about such things. But, he is very concerned with the way the Hussien Organization operates."

I was told that the basic organization holds a slave auction once a year in Morocco, where masters can sell their slaves or a slave can sell himself, for a period of 5 years. At the end of the 5 year contract the slave is free or he is returned to his master. If a master sells his slave he gets 50% of the selling price after the contract is completed and this slave gets 50% to be held in two different trusts, until he completes his contract. The slave will get half of his money at the end of his contract and the other half is held in a personal trust for him until he reaches the age of 40. If the slave sells himself he gets 50% after completion of his contract and the rest is held in trust.

But, the way the Hussien Organization operates they will write the contract that sells the slave for life in order to bring a higher price. When the slave fails to show up to collect his trust papers after the 5 year contract is up, the Hussien Organization works a new angle. The Hussien's, up until recently, had a man on the inside of the organization that helped to handle the trusts. The man would forge papers, as if the ex slave had applied for his trusts and than he would transfer the funds to the Hussiens. This inside man I have been told has been put out of business.

The Hussien slaves are either sold to a master who will keep him for life or he is sold to a master who is known as the Dutchman. The Dutchman is said to be a long haired, good looking, blond man in his 30's. Any slave sold to the Dutchman will not live more than a few years. He is a torture master and cold blooded killed. I'm sorry to say that the Dutchman is the main buyer of slaves trained by the Hussiens. You are lucky that you are not a blond or red headed young man. The Dutchman will buy any Hussien slave that has blond or red hair. The Dutchman's slaves are in for a very cruel and short life. Such slaves seldom live for more than 5 years.

After the Captain had described the Dutchman and his love of blond haired young men my jaw dropped. It had to be the same man. He was the same brutal man who claimed the young, blond slave after the auction. Man I am really glad that I wasn't sold to that crazy bastard.

"So far young man you are the only Hussien slave that I know of who has ever returned from being sold into slavery. No wonder Carlos was so shocked to see you. Carlos has sold at least 17 young men into slavery so far and it has made him a very rich young man. But, with your help I can finally start to put an end to Carlos's little business."

The Captain than paid Carlos a compliment of sorts, "You know, I hate people like Carlos, but I must admit he has talent. He can spot a true submissive, young gay man, in any type of location and he can con him into either letting him train him as a daddy's boy or a total slave. With the daddy's boy types like you, he and his relatives, in Morocco, will run a very convincing con job on them to get them to volunteer to become a slave. If Carlos collars a young man who is a slave type he will train him for total slavery himself.

Before he left, the Captain took down some information on me and he told me not to leave town until I first talked to him. He would be in contact with me and he was certain that he would soon have enough evidence on Carlos to arrest him.

That night I didn't sleep very well. I kept having dreams of Carlos and his relatives tracking me down and making sure that I did not testify again him in court.

The next morning, the Captain phoned me. He said that I need not worry about Carlos any longer, he had been found dead in an alley way, a few blocks from the bar. It seems someone had a personal score to settle with him. He had been shot three times in the crotch and than he was finished off, with a shot in the forehead.

After I hung up the phone, my mind flashed back to the night before when I saw a blond haired young man following Carlos. Up until now I didn't think that what I saw was important. Was the blond young man one of Carlos's slaves? Was there another survivor?

I did not tell the Captain about the blond young man. If one of Carlos's victims had made it back alive and killed Carlos I wasn't going to tell anyone about it. I just hoped that it was the young man I saw brutally claimed by his new master after the auction. I could well understand why a young man that was sold to the Dutchman would have a burning desire to kill Carlos.

About a week after Carlos died I got another phone call from the Captain. What the Captain told me pretty well confirmed my suspensions about the blond haired, young man that I saw following Carlos the night that he was killed. It seems the man known as the Dutchman was also dead. The Captain said that his source in the organization had told him that one of the Dutchman's slaves had killed him. What than happened to the slave in unclear.

I smiled, when I hear that the Dutchman was dead and I didn't add anything to the conversation. But, I think that the Captain suspected that there was another survivor.

The Captain told me I was now free to go, but I should let him know how to get hold of me. I felt like a big burden had been lifted off of my shoulders. For the first time in more than a month I felt safe and at ease. But, I was soon to learn that this feeling of bliss was not going to last long.

Chapter 14:

THE DECISION

It has now been 3 months since I found out about Carlos, the love of my life, was just a very talented con artist. Carlos may have been a fraud, but he did change my life in a very real way. I now have trouble thinking like an average, normal person. I have found it hard to adjust to the realities of average everyday life.

During my first few weeks in Paris, I couldn't even think of having a regular job. The idea of working at a regular 8 hour a day job didn't interest me at all. Just running my new life as a free man had become more complicated than I had expected. I have money in the bank so I don't really worry about how I am going to make a living. Well at least not right now.

My years of slavery on the island have had quiet an effect on my mind. My body is in Paris, but my mind and heart were still serving my late master. It was like I was being pulled between two completely different worlds and I still don't know which one I really belong in.

By day I walk around the streets of Paris like a regular tourist, seeing the sites and eating in small cafes. At night I worked out in a gym to keep my self fit and three nights a week I have a part time job as a stripper in a gay night club. It seems that my life is still completely centered around my body and my big dick. Some things never change.

At night, after I got off of work, I usually just go back to my hotel. Not that I don't get some interesting offers for sex and entertainment from good looking and sometimes very wealthy men, but I'm not really turned on by the usual gay social scene. Every hot man that I meet is either not dominant enough or they are phonies who are only acting the part. Most men I am just afraid to take a chance on him.

While I had a lot of opportunities to have sex, I have chosen not too. My body is free but my mind and cock were still enslaved. I had been well trained to sexually please a master and not myself. I had become very content with only getting to cum once a month.

I know that my life is a mess. I am a submissive personality with no strong man in my life. That pretty well sums up my present life. At times, late at night, in my room I get so frustrated that I just kneel submissively on the floor and repeat over and over again, "I am a slave. I exist only to serve and please my master. I am a ..." I will repeat this phrase over and over as if saying it will bring back my master and he will take me away from this new reality that scares me so much. It never happened of course and as the weeks passed I repeated this ritual less and less.

Was I beginning to find my way back to the real world again? Well I never got the chance to find out. Early one morning I checked my e-mail and found a message from Karl. The message said, "Jimmy I've got bad news. Yesterday, I saw those two red-haired goons that work for our late master's brother in Berlin. They were looking for me! If they are looking for me they are looking for you too. I am in a safe place. They will not find me. If they were able to find where I live they can find you. I will keep in contact. Good Luck Karl."

The message sent a shock wave though my body and my hands began to shake. I had thought that the trouble with those two goons was a thing of the past. Now the past was coming back along with the idea that I was being chased by a new version of the grim reaper.

As if my life was not messed up enough already I now had to deal with the fact that two hitmen wanted to kill me. The whole idea was just too much for me to handle. I sat down on the floor, with my back against the wall and cried as my whole body shook. I didn't go out that night. I just took off my clothes and crawled into bed and tried to get some sleep. I thought that maybe in the morning I would think of what I was to do.

Early the next morning, as I started to wake up, I sensed that something was not right. I had a scary feeling that I was not alone. Suddenly, the bed covers were ripped off my naked body and a pair of hands grabbed my shoulders. My whole body tensed up and I started to scream when I heard a voice, "Hello free boy." I slowly turned around and saw Karl smiling at me. As my body relaxed I said, "Well it's only you Karl. You scared the shit out of me. I thought you were those two goons from the island."

Karl just laughed, "No, I gave them the slip a few days ago in Berlin. We are both safe for a while. How long I don't know. But I have figured out what we should do about them. Karl now moved his hands down to play with my bare ass. It felt good to have a man that I trusted play with me again. "Well sweet cheeks are you open for business? I'm as horny as hell and I could sure use a good ride."

I looked at Karl and smiled, "Yes Sir!" Karl than got up and started to take off his clothes. As he let his pants fall to the floor his hard and throbbing cock slapped against his stomach. Just as he had said he was hot and horny. I put a pillow under my hips and laid my head down on the mattress and smiled. Man, after all of these frustrating months I was finally going to get fucked by an experienced top.

I relaxed as Karl spread my cheeks and I started to feel a big greased cock probe my asshole. Suddenly, Karl drove his cock deep into my ass in one stroke. My body tensed up and I moaned as Karl started to take long deep strokes. With each stroke Karl fucked me harder and harder. My whole body started to squirm. I spread my arms out on the mattress and I became lost in my own thoughts. Man it felt so good to have a big man cock up my ass again. This is what I was born to do, get royally fucked.

After about 15 minutes Karl's body started to squirm and he gritted his teeth just before he shot a big load up my ass. But Karl did not stop he just continued to fuck me. Karl was doing the same thing he liked to do back on the island he was seeing how many times he could get off while fucking my pretty ass.

Karl fucked me for over 2 hours and he shot his load 4 times. When he got close to cumming the fourth time Karl turned me over on my back. As Karl started to cum he told me to, "Cum boy, shot your load." I was so horny I didn't even have to touch my cock I just shot off a big load on my stomach at the same time Karl was shooting another load up my ass.

As Karl's spent cock slowly slid out of my ass he leaned forward and gave me a deep kiss. I ran my hands over his sweaty body and I enjoyed the feel of a man's warm tongue in my month. It had been a long time since I had such good sex, but it was worth the wait.

After we took a shower and getting dressed Karl offered to take me out to eat. After such hot sex I was eager to eat about anything. Karl picked up a briefcase and told me to follow him. He said that he knew of a nice little café that had great food and that he needed to talk to me about what we were going to do.

As we both walked through the lobby of the hotel the desk clerk, who I had become friends with, motioned that he wanted to talk to me. "Jimmy you had two visitors about an hour ago. They looked like trouble so I told them that you had moved out suddenly, yesterday. Did I do the right thing?" What he had said shook me up a little and I had to relax a little before answering. "Were they two husky red haired dudes?" The clerk just knotted his head in agreement. "Yes, you did the right thing." I than gave his a good tip for his help.

The café was only a few blocks from my hotel. All the way to the café I keep looking over the people on the streets expecting to see the two goons from the island. Thankfully, I didn't see either of them. Karl picked out an out door table for us that had no one near by. After we ordered some food Karl began to talk. "Well sweet cheeks we have a little time to talk before the food gets here. After talking to a few very powerful people I have been offered a way to solve our problems. I'm referring to our goon problem and what we are going to do with our lives."

"In regards to my present situation. I have a trust to support me from my days as a slave. I have no real money problems. But, I do have a problem of what to do to occupy my S and M mind set. No matter how hard I try I can't get my mind off of the master/slave world. It is a part of me and I doubt it will ever change. So it was a god sent when the head man of the organization offered me a job that I want and one that really suits me. The job is training slaves for the organization, which is a subject I know a lot about. In order to start the job and become a member of the organization I must satisfy only one requirement." Karl stopped talking for a moment and looked directly into my eyes. I felt my body tense up. I know what was coming. "I must sign you up for another 5 year slave contract."

Karl kept quiet for a few minutes and just let me think about what he had told me. "Karl you mean that the organization wants to put me on the block again?" "Well, not exactly. The head of the organization Mr. Bronson wants to buy you and he is offering one million dollars to buy you for the next five years He thinks that you are the best submissive that the organization has ever sold and he wants to add you to his stable. God knows you did bring the highest price ever paid for a slave when you were put on the block."

"I know that Mr. Bronson is a really hot master, but I am a little scared of him." Karl looked a little confused. "You mean you are afraid of being happy? Both of Mr. Bronson's slaves worship him. One of them has already signed his second contract and the other is on his third contract. They seem very content with their lot."

"It's just that all the time I have been a slave there was always a part of my mind that was still free. That part was what was left of the former me. Mr. Bronson is an expert slave trainer. He can really get inside of a slave's mind and mentally reshape him into a total submissive. I know if I sell myself to Mr. Bronson I will never be free again."

"You always did have a problem with making major decisions concerning your life. Remember several masters have told you that you were born to be a man's property. Wake up Jimmy fate is knocking and it is time to open the door."

I knew that Karl was right and that I owed my life to him. I could not turn him down. My fate was being decided for me. I was meant to be Mr. Bronson's property. It was actually a form of relief. I now knew what my place in the world was meant to be. My master's were right I am a born slave and my fate was to kneel naked at the feet of my master.

Karl handed me the contract. I briefly looked it over and than signed my life over to the control of Mr. Bronson. Karl put the contract in his brief case and than made a brief phone call. He than told me. "Mr. Bronson is very pleased to welcome you to his family and that he will handle our goon problem. The money will be deposited in a Swiss trust account for you. Mr. Bronson is on a business trip for now he will pick you up at my farm in about a week."

"Until than I will be your master and I intend to fuck the shit out of you every day until I have to give you up to your new master I will make the most out of this opportunity. This may be the last time I ever have the chance to fuck you and you are the best fuck I have ever had."

At that moment I started to smile. I started to really look forward to the next week with Karl and my life as Mr. Bronson's new slave. I would not be coming back to the real world. Hell, my life could be a lot worst than serving a master that really turns me on. A feeling of contentment and relief started to flow through my body. I knew that I was now safe and I finally had a real home again.

About the Author

RICHARD ANDREWS

Richard Andrews is a prolific writer of gay erotic fiction. He has had numerous short stories published in such gay magazines as Mandate, Torso and Honcho. He is an English teacher and he resides in Los Angeles.